# WHO WAS JOSEPH PULITZER?

A Novel

By Terrence Crimmins

Published by Knollwood Press, Boston, Massachusetts

ISBN: 978-0-9913783-1-9

Dedicated to:

Alan Lawson

# Table of Contents

# Foreword

Today, the public sits in awe of men like Ted Turner and Rupert Murdoch, who dominate major changes in the way news is broadcast toward the world. In the late 1800s there were very similar men, and Joseph Pulitzer was one. His life, as this novel attempts to illustrate, is the fascinating tale of a man who rose from nothing to dominate the newspaper industry of his day. Yet he was only one of a group of unique characters who helped to create what we now call the Fourth Estate, a group of men who each made their own contributions to the foundations of American journalism. Many events depicted here are recreations of actual events that occurred back in the day, and many came out of my own imagination. Sometimes, when you read a good biography, you have a feeling you know the person whose life you read about. Then, if you read another biography of one of their contemporaries, you wonder what these two individuals might have said to each other when they met. Many scenes in the book, to the best of my ability, represent the emotional conflicts of these men, and though they might not have happened in real time, they depict the feelings and conflicts these men had toward each other, when they trod the stage of the planet earth.

I could not have written the book without the excellent biographies of WA Swanberg, and Richard O'Connor, as well as period histories by too many other historians to mention. Also due my gratitude are many distinguished professors from the hallowed halls of academia who showed me the grand adventure of history from long ago. That adventure is still very much alive.

# Chapter 1

# Beginnings

Joseph Pulitzer began his career as a journalist in post-Civil War St. Louis, Missouri, a brawling young city still, like most of America, rife with the tensions that followed the end of hostilities in that bitter conflict over slavery. For anyone who has ever watched a Western movie it's easy to imagine the scenario, with horse carriages being the main mode of transportation on dirt roads beside occasional wooden sidewalks, and boots were worn as protection from the perpetual appearance of mud. Pistol packing was common, as were duels and fights for manly honor in and outside of the often crowded saloons. Most Americans still lived on farms so city life was in its infancy, compared to the way we know it today, and the people in the city lived much like the people of the country, with guns and knives often at the ready. Blacksmiths were the predominant mechanics of the day and, as we will see, they had a firm hand in the power arrangements of the urban political machine. Politics was also different because the Democratic Party was still the rural, states' rights, formerly pro-slavery party of Andrew Jackson. The Bourbon Democrats, as they were called, were resentful of the intrusion of the Republican Party of Abraham Lincoln. Lincoln's Party's attempt, under the Radical Republicans, to bring about racial equality in the South during Reconstruction touched a raw nerve in the gut of the still racist post-war South. Though at the start of our story Pulitzer was a staunch supporter of the Republicans and Abraham Lincoln, he would, eventually, switch to the Democrats, and point that party away from the farmers of rural America toward the immigrants and the cities as a source of political support. In this, as in many other issues, however, Pulitzer was ahead of his time, and the Democratic Party did not really follow his directions effectively until twenty years after his death. At the start of our story, though, Joseph Pulitzer was low on the totem pole of political power in the St. Louis of 1867.

\* \* \* \* \* \* \* \*

Pulitzer, a cub newspaper reporter, was walking down Main Street of St. Louis, on his way to a meeting of reporters at a saloon. His stroll, it is safe to say, was not pleasant. Other reporters were following him and, as they liked to do, were making fun of him, for he was a fairly recent Jewish looking immigrant with a strong Hungarian accent.

"That's Jewseph Pulitzer," said one.

"You mean Joey the Jew," said another.

"Naw, he's Pull It Sir," said yet another, sarcastically pulling at his nose.

Pulitzer forged onward, trying to keep his temper down amidst the cascade of anti-Semitic insults. He was six feet four inches tall and very skinny, with thick glasses perched at the end of a long nose. He would not be a formidable adversary in a fist fight.

"Hey Joey, your mother says it's time for bed."

"His English isn't very good."

"It's time to go back to Germany, Joseph."

Joseph, mounting the steps to the dining room of the establishment, returned fire.

"I'm from Hungary, you idiot!"

"He says he's hungry."

"Mommy must not have given him dinner."

Pulitzer stomped into the restaurant, wishing these buffoons would go away, but of course, they would not. His fellow reporters were, at that point, a proverbial lodestone around his neck. On top of that, a lively crowd of manly men were imbibing whiskey in the bar room adjoining the restaurant, and there another enemy awaited him. It was Edward Augustine, who clutched a copy of a newspaper containing an article Pulitzer had written exposing him as a corrupt judge. Augustine, actually, was more of a contractor than a judge, but had a very convenient position as a judge on the County Court to award himself contracts. He was perturbed, to say the least, that Pulitzer had pointed this out. As a contractor, he was a strong and burly man, and he discarded his drink to confront the beanpole Pulitzer, and stormed toward him.

"Let's see if you have the kind of guts in public that you do at the paper, Pulitzer," he fumed.

"You are both a liar and a crook, Mr. Augustine, and by the time I'm done with you you're going to wish you'd never come to St. Louis."

Before Pulitzer could add on to this sally Augustine seized him by the lapels and hurled him into the wall, and the thin Hungarian collapsed on the floor before rising to his knees to look up at the bully, who now had his fists up in the boxing pose. Pulitzer, realizing he had no chance in such an encounter, decided to flee, and stumbled to his feet before scurrying out of the door that he had come in, and hustled away down the street.

"You're not going to dare write about me like that again, you little pipsqueak!" Augustine blared after him.

Pulitzer rushed toward the rooming house where he was living seething with passions of revenge. On the way, he had a telling remark to make to a reporter on his way into the meeting.

"Stick around and you'll have a real story to write about," he said, without waiting for a response.

Pulitzer galloped up the stairs to his bedroom and burst into his room, searching his meager possessions for a pistol he owned. He made sure that it was loaded, and retraced the route from whence he'd come. When he reentered the restaurant Augustine again turned to confront him.

"Back for more, you little sissy?!" he cried out, storming forward.

But Pulitzer raised and cocked his pistol, in a rather clumsy fashion, allowing the men who surrounded Augustine to close in upon the attacker, and push his shooting arm downward, so the shot only grazed Augustine's leg, who fell to the floor in a not a very pleasant mood.

"You goddamn little bastard, you coward, you sneaky little dog. This ain't gonna be the end of this, I'll tell you that!"

As the manly men took their hero away Pulitzer was disarmed by others, and then taken aside by his suddenly silent reporter acquaintances, two of whom escorted him to the Police Station.

\* \* \* \* \* \* \* \*

The next day Pulitzer sat in shame at his newspaper, the Westliche Post, facing the music in a meeting with his bosses.

"It's so damn unfair, Mr. Schurz! These people are government sponsored crooks."

"Yes, Joseph, I couldn't agree with you more. But our job at the newspaper is to stay above the fray, not get down in the gutter and fight with them," Schurz replied.

Schurz was a German immigrant who had escaped from jail after the Revolution there in 1848, and came to America to become a farmer. But then the Civil War intervened, and Schurz did more than his duty for the Union Army, rising to the rank of General. He was also a well-educated man and decided, after the war, to put his learning to use in the newspaper business.

"Don't I have the right to defend myself?" Pulitzer cried out.

"You defend yourself with the newspaper, Joseph, not a gun."

"The real weapon Joseph, is that little notebook that you carry around," interjected his other boss, Thomas Davidson.

Davidson was not actually a newspaper man but a professor of philosophy, another immigrant from Germany. But he had grown tired of academia and wanted to do something closer to ordinary people. He was a very kind man, and saw that Pulitzer was very intelligent, but also a young man of strong feelings. He would come to be a mentor for the struggling young immigrant, who would grow, in time, to be Davidson's employer.

\* \* \* \* \* \* \* \*

Joseph sat grimly at a pre-trial hearing in the Municipal Court of St. Louis shaking in his boots, as they say, afraid that Mr. Augustine would succeed in putting him in jail. Of course he had to plead self-defense, and who would not believe it, Pulitzer thought, if they'd seen the way that bully had thrown him against the wall like a sack of flour. There were other aspects of the story that were the reasons for his shaking—reasons Pulitzer himself did not enjoy thinking about that would lead toward attempted murder. In Pulitzer's heart, however, this man was a public villain of the worst order so his own actions, faulted though they were, were in the public interest. Such being the case a little liberty with the facts was not unwarranted, with the added benefit of keeping him from going to jail.

The courtroom was divided in half by those parties who were sympathetic to the two sides. The halves were only regarding physical space, however, as the much larger half of spectators sat behind Augustine, with many of the belligerent manly men who had been with him in the saloon on that night. Their side reveled in a clear expectation of the imminent revenge of justice upon this upstart pipsqueak that they so despised. Pulitzer's section was much smaller, unfortunately for him, consisting of Schurz, Davidson, and only three of the clique of reporters who were there on the night of the alleged attack, evidencing the fact that Augustine's proponents were not the only people who had written off the future of Joseph Pulitzer. The two sides did, however, comprise the two sides in the battle for control of St. Louis: the Bourbon Democrats and their powerful political machine versus a new and lowly group of newspaper reporters. The odds-makers in Vegas, it might be presumed, would not have given the reporters much of a chance.

Augustine approached the bench to present his case in a state of slightly restrained anger, with his right pants leg rolled up to show the bandage from the shooting. In this court of law with the blind maiden of justice, thought Augustine, surely he would prevail, so he had confidence this little whippersnapper would be off to prison, for some time, and surely, with a criminal record, never return to being a reporter. Being a newspaper reporter was a tasteless job for sissies and weasels, and such panty-waists that were in charge there would never offer someone a job who had a criminal record.

"And so, Your Honor," the fraudulent judge said to the presiding Judge, finishing up his case, "only the actions of my friends in restraining him saved my life."

When his turn came Joseph Pulitzer meekly approached the bench with feelings of greatest alarm, for the deck seemed stacked against him. He attempted to amplify his case for self-defense by casting himself as the victim of a most ruthless bully.

"Mr. Augustine has mentioned some of the facts, Your Honor, but he left out how he verbally threatened me because of some reporting I had done about him," the judge gave a knowing nod, "and then picked me up and threw me against the wall. I rose, your honor, and when I looked at Mr. Augustine, he raised his hand up in the air and he was holding something gold, your honor, which I thought looked like a gun."

"That's bullshit, Your Honor!"

The judge banged the gavel.

"Mr. Augustine, as *you* should be well aware," he paused, with a cool glare at the corrupt judge, "this is a court of law, requiring decorum. If you use profanity again I will hold you in contempt. In addition, sir, you were allowed to present your case without interruption, so please allow Mr. Pulitzer to do the same. Please proceed Mr. Pulitzer."

The insides of Joseph Pulitzer suddenly felt a spark. Could it be that the worm had turned? He felt a sudden rise in his standing before the court.

"And so, Your Honor, I thought that what he was holding might be a gun, so that I had to act in self-defense."

Pulitzer sat down. His adversary glared at him, and the judge had to bang the gavel to quiet the grumblings of protest amongst the grossly offended Augustine supporters. Pulitzer stared ahead timidly, as the judge ruminated the case, surmising the size differential between the two opponents.

"The Court rules that the Defendant acted in self-defense," ruled the judge. "There will be no trial.

Mr. Pulitzer must pay the court costs, however, of one hundred dollars."

The Judge then brought down his gavel with a resounding whack, and abruptly rose to leave the courtroom.

"All rise," intoned the Bailiff.

There was no doctor present to measure the rise in blood pressure of Mr. Augustine, but it was precipitous. This was evidenced by the much redder color on his face, his apoplectic rise to his feet, and slightly restrained stamping and glaring at the departing judge. Joseph Pulitzer grinned gleefully with immense relief as he firmly shook the hands of Carl Schurz and Thomas Davidson. He clearly understood their non-verbal language however because his bosses' facial expressions clearly said you've gotten away with something and are not blameless, Cub Reporter.

Who can say whether the decision by the Judge was somewhat political because he believed, like Pulitzer, that Augustine was a public crook who should be removed from his position as a Judge? Whatever the reason for the decision, however, one thing is clear. Had he decided the other way, in all probability, the journalistic career of Joseph Pulitzer would have come to an abrupt end.

Joseph and his partisans left the courtroom somewhat quietly, under the self-righteous glare of their opponents on the Augustine side, trying to keep their chins up despite some of the foul and indiscrete insults being cast in their direction. Without the Judge there to restrain them anymore the manly men felt free to broadcast their opinions, and the Bailiff did nothing to intervene. The battle lines were clearly drawn.

\* \* \* \* \* \* \* \*

Many readers must be curious about how Joseph Pulitzer got into this position, so let's do a little background. Americans love a rags to riches story, and Pulitzer's is that, or almost that. His is a riches-to-rags-to-riches story, for he came from a wealthy family in Hungary to the Unites States where he experienced poverty before pulling himself up by his own bootstraps to become wealthy again.

Pulitzer grew up in a town called Mako, a suburb of Budapest, Hungary, where his father was a successful Jewish businessman. But his father died young, and Pulitzer's mother had difficulty maintaining the business she had inherited as a widow, and remarried to rescue her family from the threat of poverty. This marriage did not please the young Joseph Pulitzer, however, who hated his new stepfather, and who was so angry about it he blew up in the receiving line at his mother's remarriage ceremony.

"I cannot stand it," the young firebrand exclaimed to his Uncle Henri.

"Don't be silly, Joseph, your new father is a very nice man, and now he's your stepfather. You'll grow to like him."

"I hate him."

"Come now Joseph, you're young, and I'm sure you miss your Father, but what would he want, eh? Would he want you to be like this?"

"Are you crazy?! He would not want Mother to remarry! It is dishonorable for her to remarry as a widow."

"I didn't mean it that way, Joseph, I mean—"

"I won't stand for it, I'm telling you, and I'm leaving."

"You're leaving? Don't be silly, Joseph. You can't leave now."

"Oh yes I can."

"You can't possibly leave now, Joseph, for goodness sakes, where on earth are you going to go?"

"I am leaving this instant and I am going to join the army."

Joseph left the receiving line and strutted down a side hallway of the castle-like building. His brother Albert, four years his junior at thirteen, snitched on his older brother.

"Mommy, look! Joseph says that he is leaving to join the army!"

Their mother gazed pessimistically at the departing adolescent.

"Shall I go get him?" inquired Uncle Henri.

"Let him go," the stoic mother replied.

\* \* \* \* \* \* \* \*

Pulitzer faced several disadvantages in his attempt to join the army, however, most being physical. He looked a bit odd in the recruiting office in Vienna, where his emaciated, stork-like figure, large nose and thick eyeglasses put him in an unenviable position.

"You're too thin," the officer harangued, "not strong enough, and couldn't see the broad side of a barn without those glasses."

"But I could do it, I tell you," the young tyro protested.

"Forget it, we won't take you. Next!"

An angry Joseph Pulitzer stormed away.

He would not take no for an answer, however, and sought to join the French Army, but encountered similar difficulties in the Paris recruiting office.

"He's so thin he'd be hard to shoot," the officer said to his fellow recruiter.

"Maybe he could be a coat rack."

"I think he'd be better as a scarecrow."

"He might scare a small sparrow."

"Are you going to take me or not!?" the determined young man demanded.

"Take you? You must be kidding."

"Next!"

Pulitzer stormed out of another recruiting office.

He crossed the English Channel hoping a better fate awaited him there, but it proved a disappointment, though an officer at least afforded counseling.

"Look mate, not everyone is meant to be a soldier."

"But I could do it!" the bug-eyed Pulitzer postulated.

"Go back home, there's other careers for ya."

"I can do it, I tell you."

"There's other things you'd be perfectly good at..."

Pulitzer did not want to waste his time listening to an extrapolation of this theory, and once again, he stomped out the door.

In frustration, he went to Frankfort, Germany, and, on a chance, ended up in a recruiting office of the Union Army, who were searching desperately for soldiers to fight in the American Civil War. Pulitzer was unaware that they would take just about any living breathing male on the planet to get the bounty that the government paid for recruits crossing the Atlantic Ocean.

"Of course we'll take you," an officer informed him.

"You will?" Pulitzer inquired, dumbfounded.

"Indeed we will," a second officer told him. "We need soldiers to fight to restore the Union."

"Can you ride a horse?" the first officer inquired.

"I am an expert horse rider!" exclaimed Pulitzer energetically. "I can canter, gallop, jump fences—"

"Fine, fine, we'll put you in the Cavalry. Welcome to the Union Army."

Pulitzer stood to salute proudly.

"Next!"

He was greeted with cursory salutes, and shunted off again.

\* \* \* \* \* \* \*

On the crowded ship across the Atlantic, Pulitzer learned new things about the United States. From a German emigrant he discovered that the bounty money they were supposed to get was going to be pilfered by other selfish individuals. One of the Planet Earth's oldest traditions, government corruption, was clearly in play.

"I am not going to stand for it!" Pulitzer exclaimed, beginning a style of rebellion that would be his own life-long tradition.

Standing on the bow of the ship in New York Harbor, Pulitzer took matters into his own hands and dived overboard. Thus a seventeen year old runaway who barely spoke English made his entry into the United States. He swam to shore, found the recruiting office for the Lincoln New York Cavalry, identified himself, collected the bounty, and registered for what he hoped would be a dynamic career in the Union Army.

Here fate again disappointed him, as his unusual physique, strong accent and peculiar eye-wear made him an easy scapegoat. Men being what they are, especially young men, in the army, thrown together so quickly in close companionship, are liable to pick on people who stand out as different from themselves, and Pulitzer was that. The young foreigner was intelligent, as the future would show but, in the army, he could not demonstrate it, nor did his very limited proficiency with English help his cause. In such circumstances Pulitzer was easily frustrated, and one incident got him into trouble, on a day when he rode his horse back into camp in Manassas, Virginia.

"Back from the front so soon, Fritzy?" a soldier queried as Pulitzer tied up his horse.

"My name is Joseph!"

"Aw, come on, Fritzy," another soldier admonished.

"You look like a Fritzy," asserted a third.

"And you sound like a Fritzy," postulated a fourth.

But Pulitzer had heard enough, and sucker punched the closest man, who was a non-commissioned officer, which was a capital offense. A higher officer, however, felt compassion for the young immigrant, and argued to his senior officers as to the somewhat unfair difficulties of the young Hungarian. He saved Pulitzer's neck, so to speak, and took him on as his orderly after he finished his term in the brig. This may have been, at least in part, because he had difficulty finding a chess partner in the army, a game that Pulitzer played with flare. So Pulitzer finished the war in a bureaucratic role while other adventurous men fought the mighty cavalry battles that General Phil Sheridan engaged in to corner Robert E. Lee at the end of the Civil War.

When the war was over Pulitzer, like tens of thousands of other Civil War veterans, was dumped back into New York City where he trod the streets looking for work. As is often the case after a major war there was a post-war recession, contributed to because the factories were no longer so busy making weapons and the sudden enlargement of the work force of the returning soldiers created a difficult economic climate. Unable to find a lasting job, Pulitzer took what turned out to be a short trip to New Bedford, Massachusetts, to investigate the whaling industry. There he found he had nothing in common with Herman Melville, at least regarding a desire for that adventurous job in his youth because he found the possibility of getting on a whaling boat a dangerous and degrading proposition. Returning to New York he continued to plod the streets looking for work becoming, in time, almost homeless, and desperate for a career path. Yet even in his lowest condition he continued to go to the French Hotel to get his shoes shined, to maintain at least a semblance of respectability, but the patrons there did not enjoy his presence, and he was advised to get his threadbare self out of the establishment for good. Who could have known this hotel was in the same neighborhood where Pulitzer would, some twenty years later, become one of the most influential newspapermen in modern history.

However, Pulitzer heard tales of a large German population in St. Louis, and thought that such a city might welcome him more than the places he had tried so far, so he cast his fate in that direction. To get there, he had to sell his last remaining valuable possession, a silk scarf, which he did in a clothing shop in a Jewish Ghetto on Manhattan. On a crowded street of Kosher Delis, meat stores, Jewish bookstores teeming with Jewish immigrants like himself, Pulitzer dickered with the proprietor about the value of his possession.

"Seventy-five cents?" he exclaimed. "It is certainly worth more than that!"

"Yer not sellin' it from a store, kid, you're bartering it. Sorry, that's all you get."

"It's silk! And look at the hand stitching!"

The tradesman noticed a gold chain around Pulitzer's neck.

"Hey, what's that chain? That I might give you something for. Has it got a locket?"

It had a locket, with a picture of Pulitzer's mother, one of his most prized possessions, which he kept close at hand until his dying day.

"Yes," he replied unenthusiastically.

"Let me at least have a look."

"Okay," and he pulled it out to give him a glance, not taking it off.

"Your mother?"

Pulitzer nodded.

"Okay, my boy, I will not attempt to make you part with that. Listen, I'll give you eighty cents for the scarf."

"Oh come on, it's worth a dollar at least."

"Eighty cents is it, and a nickel too much," the man enjoined calmly, wiping the counter. "Take it or leave it."

Pulitzer grumbled, and nodded, handing the scarf over. The fellow watched him march off.

"Good luck in St. Louis," he said, as the future newspaper magnate departed.

\* \* \* \* \* \* \* \*

Young Pulitzer had a difficult train ride across the eastern United States, shivering severely in the early spring cold. Someone, unfortunately, had stolen his Army greatcoat. Such was his impoverished condition as he surveyed the nation he had fought to unify, gazing out the boxcar at the cornfields, forests and cities on those chilly early March days. When he was put off of the train he found further difficulties, as he had to cross the mighty Mississippi River to get to St. Louis, and hadn't the funds to pay for his passage on the ferry. He talked his way into a position to feed the boiler for several trips back and forth, and stooped down with a shovel to heave coal into the fires of a ferry chugging across the river that Mark Twain would immortalize in The Adventures of Huckleberry Finn.

St. Louis did not seem like the promised land, to Pulitzer, for a couple of years, as he worked a succession of odd jobs in order to eke out a living, such as selling steam boat tickets, driving a hansom cab, construction work and, at one point, caring for a brace of mules. He later joked that someone who has never had to care for mules does not know what work and troubles are. Judging from his behavior and disposition, one would probably bet this was an occupation that Pulitzer stormed away from in a huff. Here, in his early days, we can see elements of the personality that characterized Pulitzer throughout his entire life. He had a huge ambitions and a lofty opinion of himself as a man who could achieve great things, and in this he was correct. He was also very sensitive, did not take orders well, and was what we would today call a control freak. Pulitzer had an ego that made him feel he could do things better than other men, and considered it a gross injustice when any other occupant of the planet earth ever questioned his judgment, especially when they were telling him what to do. Because of this he was prone to mood swings, as he, whether he liked it or not, was certainly subject to many forces outside of his control, and this he found frustrating. Today we might call Pulitzer bi-polar, but at that time there was little or no counseling to deal with such a problem, except for, perhaps, organized religion, to which Pulitzer had little or no connection.

Despite these emotional problems, though, Pulitzer began his rapid ascent from his lowly economic status through the hard work and ruthless ambition he had throughout his life. When he was not working he spent almost all of his time reading at the public library, becoming a self-taught man who not only learned the intricacies of the English language, but passed an exam to obtain a law license. Poring over books as though someone was about to snatch them away, Pulitzer pursued a love of the classics that would make him a well-read man.

It was during this period, when he worked as a waiter in a popular restaurant/barroom, that he first met Carl Schurz and Thomas Davidson, who were regular customers there. Between serving things he would stop to chat with them, as he did one eventful day. On that day, Schurz and Davidson were having lunch with Peter Kepler, a cartoonist who later made himself famous by creating a magazine called Puck. Pulitzer, adapting more and more through his labors at the library to his new land, was able to engage in intellectual small talk with these prominent citizens of St. Louis.

"We still haven't decided if Thomas here is a heretic. What do you think, Joseph?"

"Maybe he's a philosophical heretic," Pulitzer replied.

"That's negative, Carl, you sound prejudiced against me," Davidson rejoined.

"No, I'm not prejudiced, just skeptical," said Schurz.

"How do you define yourself, Thomas?" asked Kepler.

"Well, if I'm a heretic, I'm an enlightened heretic, and my desire is how to best help my fellow man."

"He sounds as though he's a helpful heretic," Pulitzer observed.

"I'm not formally religious anymore, and if that is deemed heretical, I justify my heresy by saying that I've become more interested in helping my fellow man than by proclaiming myself a man chosen by God."

"Than what you are is an independent," said Schurz.

"Get in here Pulitzer! You've got an order up!" bellowed the manager from the kitchen.

Pulitzer raised his eyebrows and departed for the kitchen.

"He seems like a bright young man," Kepler observed.

"I saw him at the library last night playing chess with someone," said Schurz.

"Really?" asked Davidson.

"Yes, and they say he's there almost every night, reading away until closing time."

"Maybe you can hire him at your paper, Carl," Kepler suggested.

"I don't know if he knows St. Louis well enough."

"I bet he'd learn fast," said Davidson.

Suddenly the trio heard a crash, and looked over to observe that the gangling Pulitzer, stumbling on his way out of the kitchen, had dropped a tray of food right onto the table of four businessmen, destroying their lunch. Pulitzer awkwardly rushed around the table trying to pick up the mess, and the men looked at him in disgust as the manager stormed over.

"That's it for you, Pulitzer, that's the last straw. Give me your checks and get out of here right now."

He grabbed Pulitzer by the elbow, and snatched the checks out of his apron pocket. After stripping the hapless Hungarian of his apron, he shoved him toward the door.

"The only time I want to see you again is when you come to pay the checks for the meals you've just destroyed, because we're going to have to cook new ones. Get out!"

Pulitzer backed up in a meek withdrawal, his eyes full fear and anger like a newly caged animal. He then turned around and retreated quickly out the door.

"I'm terribly sorry, gentlemen. We'll move you to another table, immediately. Billy! Put these men at Table 43."

"Well, well, he is going to need a job," said Kepler.

"You've got that right," agreed Schurz.

"Will you excuse me, gentlemen?" Davidson asked.

"Have something helpful to do, Thomas?" Kepler inquired.

Davidson got up and strode off in pursuit.

"I find it useful to help my fellow man," he declared over his shoulder.

"He's going to practice the golden rule like a heretic," opined Schurz.

"That should make the front page," Kepler asserted.

Davidson caught up with Pulitzer on the dirt roadway.

"Joseph, Joseph," he enjoined, reaching out to guide Pulitzer to the wooden sidewalk, where they sat down. Pulitzer had tears in his eyes.

"I can't seem to make it in any job," he lamented.

"Aw, Joseph, don't feel so bad. Being a waiter is a tough job, and there aren't many who can do it. Besides, I think we both know that you are cut out for better in life."

"Really?"

"Sure, Joseph. Some friends of mine own a law firm and they could use somebody to run errands, and maybe more. What do you think?"

"What do I think? Can I start right now?"

\* \* \* \* \* \* \* \*

So began Pulitzer's career in journalism, as he gradually transitioned from errand boy to reporter. His thick accent and bizarre frame did not help him become a successful lawyer, as clients were deterred by his language and appearance. These impediments did not matter to Pulitzer the reporter, however, where his immense curiosity and intellectual stamina made him do well. He demonstrated these qualities in two jobs he had on his way up the professional ladder. The first was taking charge of the island where the victims of a cholera epidemic were taken for burial, as Pulitzer had the courage to take the job when even prisoners chose to stay in jail rather than work there. The second was when he was put in charge of mapping out the counties of Missouri and adapting insurance regulations to them, where his prodigious memory enabled him to show organizational abilities that few could match.

But it was his curiosity as a reporter that best equipped him for a career in journalism, and he wore out the people he besieged with an endless procession of questions, often prompting them to cut the interview short while Pulitzer was still picking their brains for minor details. In doing so he became well acquainted with the politics of St. Louis of his day, and the place of his new city on the national scene. He also took a great and passionate interest in any democratic election. To Pulitzer, raised in the final days of aristocratic governments of Europe, where the people were ruled by kings allegedly chosen by God, the American democratic process was a new and wonderful experience. Not only did he revel in the electoral process, but, as we will see, took a passionate interest in who would win the elections.

The initial fulcrum he used to change the newspaper business of the United States, however, was the unflinching way he questioned the powers that be in the St. Louis Missouri of his day. Perhaps, in part, he had an advantage as an immigrant, for he did not take things for granted as Americans were more prone to do, and spotted exploitation where they would not. His perspective was a fresh eye on what we today know to be gross injustices, and he became one of the first people to point them out. In doing so, he started from the bottom up, and relentlessly marched the streets to question the people who were the foundation of the Bourbon Democratic Political Machine.

One day he interviewed a blacksmith who, as he could see from an insignia mounted on the wooden fence that enclosed his furnace, was a member of the Black Lantern, a professional/political organization that supported the state and city machine of the ruling Bourbon Democrats.

"Are you in the Dark Lantern?" he inquired.

"None of your Goddamn business!" snorted the blacksmith.

"Well I see the logo for it over there."

"I told you it's none of your Goddamn business."

"Isn't it true that you help pack the vote for certain candidates in exchange for business?"

The blacksmith pulled a red hot iron out of the fire and lunged toward Pulitzer with it.

"If you don't get out of here I'm going to stick this where the sun don't shine, asshole!"

Pulitzer jaunted away.

"I'm going to take that as a yes."

On another occasion he sought to investigate another part of the Bourbon Democrats' political empire—bordellos. These thriving establishments were part of the machine, and sometimes even the site of political parties where the machine politicians had celebrations of the electoral victories that the Black Lantern helped to engineer. Pulitzer knocked on the door as if he were a customer, and the Madame of the establishment, clad in her sporty red dress, blonde curls, bright red lipstick and fishnet stockings, asked him if he were interested.

"Why certainly I'm interested," Pulitzer replied.

"Well why don't you step right in then, fellow."

The Madame did not ask whether he was a policeman, partly because she knew that almost all of St. Louis' finest were paid off, and would not visit, and partly because of Pulitzer's appearance. On this occasion the attributes that had been a disadvantage to Pulitzer were turned the other way around, for the forewoman of the bordello immediately pigeonholed him in her imagination with such labels as nerd, geek, homely, ungainly and loser. She thought Pulitzer was just another of the parade of dolts, in her view, who frequented her establishment.

But upon entry, when Pulitzer pulled out his little notebook, her lofty impressions crashed to the ground as she suddenly realized that she had engaged in a dangerous mischaracterization.

"How many girls do you have working here?" Pulitzer inquired, surveying the line of concubines that stood lasciviously in the hallway.

"What the hell??!!" she screamed out. "George, get in here quickly and get this bum out of here."

Again Pulitzer hustled to escape, figuring he had garnered all the direct information he was going get from that establishment, as the burly bouncer pursued him.

Back at the paper, Pulitzer reported on the results of his lengthy investigation.

"The hall of records has the owners of all those houses of prostitution listed clearly, Mr. Schurz, and all we have to do is publish their names in the paper."

"You are certainly shaking things up, Joseph," his boss replied.

"Is that not what a newspaper is supposed to do, Mr. Schurz?"

Schurz nodded, but had a look of perplexity on his face, for Pulitzer was changing the way the game was played. He was not content to let things lay, as the other reporters were, and was determined to challenge the powers that be. I cannot imagine today how unusual this was, before the creation of what is now considered to be the Fourth Estate. Reporters before Pulitzer were content to play the role that people like Augustine imagined them to have, which was more like placid souls who wrote out the news like a business inventory, and would never relate sordid affairs like murder and divorce. Pulitzer saw no such limits in his new, adopted land, and neither his mind nor his heart were restricted by the social conventions that governed the behavior of his coworkers.

Schurz and Davidson observed the unusual energy of Pulitzer, who worked twelve to fourteen hours a day like a maniac, without fear or trepidation toward the people he investigated, as the near-miss with Augustine had not cooled him down. As the years went on, Pulitzer began to mature and feel more sure of himself, confronting increasingly more powerful people not only in the newspaper but in person as well, as he began to feel himself like a knight from the fables of old with a solemn duty to attack the evil powers that made common citizens powerless. Pulitzer and Davidson, however, had fears there would be new enemies on the horizon similar to Augustine who would confront the lowly young reporter, and were surprised when he continued to attack such people as their equal. When the two looked out their second floor window one afternoon, Pulitzer was hustling out of the building to pursue what he considered the dragons of democracy, they evaluated their protégé's efforts.

"He's certainly shaking things up," Davidson postulated.

"You can say that again," agreed Schurz.

"He's attacking lots of people."

"And they're going to try to do something about it."

As they spoke, coincidentally, Pulitzer was encountering opposition. As he dashed down the stairs and was confronted by a man who approached him with a much slower tread. This man was Jake Usher, a man whose own name had been published on a list in the Post as the owner of a house of prostitution. This portly middle aged fellow, the man with the appearance of someone with a body that had gone to seed for lack of exercise, struggled mightily to ascend the staircase. In doing so, he made himself a virtual roadblock as Pulitzer, who was bouncing down the stairs, and was forced to come to a halt.

"Mr. Pulitzer, we have to have a talk. My name is Jake Usher, and you published my name as an owner of a house of prostitution. I want to tell you I have no control..."

"You have to talk with me!!! Get a grip! You, the owner of a whorehouse? You are one of the worst types of criminal, worse than the lowly street thug because you disguise yourself in rich clothes to give yourself the appearance of dignity. You have no dignity you God-damn, dirty, low down scum—get out of here before I add trespassing to your crimes and rest assured, you asshole, that we will give further attention to you in our newspaper at the earliest opportunity."

Pulitzer's mighty excoriation succeeded in propelling the man downward, and he backed up as though he were encountering the winds of a mighty storm. Pulitzer, relieved of the obstruction, stepped around the man to dash off to his next conquest.

"Looks like our boy can take care of himself," Schurz observed, watching Pulitzer stride down the street.

"And a few other people, too," agreed Davidson.

* * * * * * * *

A few nights later, Pulitzer stated his broad ambitions plainly to his bosses. They sat at a table in the same bar where Pulitzer had his incident with Augustine, but his former 98-pound weakling status was now but a distant memory.

"What I'm doing is not enough, Mr. Schurz."

"Not enough?"

"We've got to raise the circulation or our crusades won't work."

"Circulation is going up."

"Not by enough," Pulitzer contended.

"What do you propose, Joseph?" Davidson inquired.

"Giving the people what they want."

Schurz and Davidson paused for a minute, struck by the audacity of Pulitzer's statement.

"And pray tell, what is that, Joseph?" Schurz inquired.

"Gossip, entertainment and scandal."

Again his bosses sat dumbfounded.

"Appealing to their lower instincts? How on earth is that going to help people, Joseph?" inquired Davidson.

"If we are going to educate them we first have to get them to read the paper. Preaching to empty pews does nothing."

Schurz and Davidson both sat back to ponder this basic truth of sensationalistic journalism. Though their traditional academic training restricted them to certain codes of conduct, they knew that the masses of mankind did not live by such strictures. Yet they had never tried to build a bridge to communicate with ordinary people, and considered the approach suggested by their protégé out of bounds. Though Pulitzer could discuss philosophy with the best, including his bosses with their academic backgrounds, he had something that they did not, an instinct for what approach would truly resonate with the public, and the fundamental importance of dramatizing the news in stark colors that the public could understand. The young Hungarian saw plainly that newspapers that were like church bulletins would make no difference, because people would either not read them or be little influenced by what they said. He realized that newspapers had to grab people by the throat, move them, and that their instincts were best roused by the base emotions that caused fights in the barrooms or gossip over the back fence. Once a paper had used such methods to attract people's attention, circulation would have a meteoric rise, and then the people could be educated on the problems that confronted them, and they then could be roused to do something about it.

Thereafter Pulitzer began to salt the front page of the paper with controversy as a way to draw in readers. Stories about divorce, murder, petty crime and scandal with lurid headlines appealed to readers in a way they could understand. Pulitzer showed that he had a deep insight into how to liven up the news and, put an electric charge of the thrill of life when people picked up the paper. And once the readers' dander was raised, they would be ready to learn about and confront the problems that caused their oppression, such as the political machines and giant corporations who at that time, had no government regulations or supervision to impede them from the kind of exploitation that is almost unimaginable today.

The other newspapers of St. Louis quickly noticed this new style of journalism, and were very skeptical whether it would have any lasting effect on their reader-base. One such paper was the Republican, an established morning daily that, at that time, ruled the roost of St. Louis papers. Its building was in a far more established section of St. Louis than the Post, and was a solid four story red brick structure with its brass logo firmly mounted on the building, a far cry from the wooden building of the Westliche Post with an insignificant wooden sign that swung back and forth in the breeze. The Republican, oddly, was really a Democratic paper because it supported the Bourbon Democrats, and the urban machine that kept them in power, including the blacksmiths' union, the Black Lantern. Content and confident of their ruling position, they did not take Pulitzer seriously when he first began to rock the boat. The editor of the paper, William Hyde, and his right hand man, Jeffrey Salem, surveyed a copy of the Post in Hyde's office when Pulitzer began to liven up the Post's coverage.

"This Pulitzer fellow seems quite ambitious," Hyde postulated.

"Yes, his presentation of the news might be called gaudy," agreed Salem.

"True."

"Did you see this? Wily Widow Robs Suitors."

"Isn't that a fine one?"

"He doesn't care what kind of cheap trash he reports," fumed the editor.

"It won't last long."

"I should hope not!"

Had these men been able to gaze into a crystal ball they would have seen visions of sensationalistic journalism, and stories that would make Pulitzer's efforts seem staid by comparison. However, they did not at all feel that his new brand of opposition was a threat, even though he was getting people to read newspapers who had not done so before. Pulitzer had made newspapers truly democratic, and raised up the common man to confront the powers that be.

But even in his own paper he was making waves, as Schurz and Davidson were somewhat bewildered by the new system that Pulitzer was inaugurating. The young man was taking more control, as time went on, and circulation was going up in the dramatic rise that Pulitzer so deeply desired. He was hiring reporters, travelling around Missouri to political conventions and meetings, and designing the layout of the entire paper. Schurz felt like a bystander. It should not, therefore, have come as a surprise to Pulitzer when Schurz called him to his office for a meeting.

"I'm going to be leaving for New York, Joseph," Schurz informed him.

"You are?" Pulitzer replied incredulously.

"I've been offered the editorship of a paper called the Evening Post."

"Congratulations."

"You are going to run the show here, Joseph."

"So soon?"

"I think that you are ready Joseph."

"Maybe, but I don't know if I can afford full owner-ship, Mr. Schurz."

"I think that we can work something out."

And so as the lawyers worked together to frame up articles of incorporation for Pulitzer and work out payments for his debt to Schurz to take control of the paper, Pulitzer realized that the paper was truly going to become his own baby. He had transformed it from an obscure sheet that catered to German Americans to a living breathing newspaper that contended for top billing with the big boys.

\* \* \* \* \* \* \* \*

Two weeks later there was a goodbye party for Schurz at his own home. It was a sunny day in June, and local dignitaries socialized on the lawn while listening to a chamber quartet while eating southern snacks from a catered buffet, next to a small bar that served wine and cocktails. Pulitzer was talking to Schurz when an attractive young lady named Kate Davis joined the conversation. She was an extremely attractive brunette from one of St. Louis's most prominent families.

"Is this the daring new reporter that the whole town is talking about?" she inquired.

"I hope the whole town isn't talking about me," rejoined Pulitzer.

"Miss Davis, Mr. Pulitzer. Mr. Pulitzer, Miss Davis."

The two exchanged greetings.

"He talks about himself a lot," Schurz quipped.

"Stop. I don't believe that for a moment. You write wonderful articles, Mr. Pulitzer."

"Why thank you, Miss Davis."

"You're going to be taking over the paper, aren't you?"

"Sort of…"

Schurz turned away, drawn into a conversation with Davidson and others.

"It is a beautiful garden here," Kate theorized.

"Indeed it is. Have you seen the azaleas?" queried Pulitzer.

"I don't believe that I have."

"They're right over here. Shall we take a look?" he said, offering her his arm.

"I'd be happy too, Mr. Pulitzer," she replied, taking his arm for the stroll.

The other guests watched as the young couple chose their own path on a walkway to the azalea garden, which was down on a lower level from the patio, somewhat away from the melodies of the quartet. They strolled around the path that skirted a group of azalea bushes that surrounded a cement bench, where they sat down.

"Do you miss Hungary?"

"Sometimes," Pulitzer responded.

"What about your family?" Kate inquired.

"My father passed away a few years ago."

"I'm sorry to hear that."

"Thank you."

Kate was curious about this young dynamo. How could such a recent immigrant as he have become so successful, so quickly?

"What about your mother?' she inquired.

"She was remarried."

"Oh?"

"I wasn't happy about it."

Kate sensed that she had touched a nerve.

"So you came over here to fight in the war."

"Pretty much," Pulitzer replied.

There was a slight pause in the conversation.

"Let me ask, if you don't mind, what is your goal, Mr. Pulitzer?"

"My goal?" he questioned, somewhat taken aback.

"What drives you? What do you hope to do as a newspaperman?"

Pulitzer meditated for a minute on how to respond to this direct query, before responding.

"To help the millions of immigrants who weren't as lucky as me."

"That is very generous of you."

"Someone has to help them get away from being exploited by the fat-cats."

Thereafter, the couple transitioned into more ordinary conversation, gossiping about the theater, music, goings on about town, and started to get to know each other.

\* \* \* \* \* \* \*

## Chapter 2

# Rising to the Top

"Listen up everybody!" Pulitzer blared out across the newsroom. "Let's start with the headline. Mr. White writes 'Clive Wedge hanged for murder.' I am afraid that that is incorrect. You don't just say that so and so got executed. First of all, he's not just a so and so, he's a killer, and we have to remind our readers of that! That is why he is being executed. So we can combine those two facts in one headline. Don't forget, condense, condense, condense, that is the essence of good reporting. A lot of news, quickly, and presented in an interesting and dramatic fashion. We want to get the thrill of life into people's veins the moment they pick up the paper. Now, Mr. White, did this man enjoy the prospect of execution?"

Frank White was a newly hired inexperienced reporter, and was being rapidly woken up to the methodology of the dominating Pulitzer, who bounced about the newsroom like Superman, attempting to galvanize his fledgling news team.

"No, Mr. Pulitzer," the cub reporter replied unsurely.

"'Killer clings to bars before execution.' That, Mr. White, is the kind of headline that gets peoples' attention."

White was latched onto a rising star in American journalism, however, and the aggressive style that he was learning would become the foundation of newspapers across the globe. As he learned from Pulitzer the new ways of getting peoples' attention the second they picked up the paper, he became part of the paper's rise to the top. Pulitzer, with the new gains in circulation, was able to pay off his debts and began to think about purchasing other papers, one of which soon came to his attention.

This other paper was called the Dispatch, edited by the cautious and conservative journalist John Dillon. Dillon followed the established practices of the newspapermen of his day, outlining the major events in a rather placid fashion. Professional life had become difficult for Dillon, however, who watched as Pulitzer's paper increased its circulation while gaining more of the kind of political influence that he had hoped for, while his own paper remained in the doldrums. So when Pulitzer came to visit him to propose a merger, Dillon cannot have helped but to feel no small measure of relief. Sitting in his comparatively meager den, Dillon responded enthusiastically to Pulitzer's suggestion.

"It's a great idea! Combining our two papers would give us a chance of being the largest paper in St. Louis," Dillon volunteered.

"We could call the paper the St. Louis Post-Dispatch. What do you think?"

Thus was created one of America's most established newspapers, though it was not clear to anyone at the time. Its transformation, of course, was geared by

Pulitzer, who did not long want to share a partnership where two men had dual control of the paper. Almost immediately after moving the apparatus of the Dispatch to the headquarters of The Post, Dillon saw that he was going to become a mere observer to the dynamic and effervescent energy that Pulitzer infected his staff with, and realized, as Schurz had, that his role would be minimal. This polite and reserved gentleman felt like a museum sculpture on the sidelines as Pulitzer cruised around the office like a shark, and realized that any suggestions he might make would be considered a step slow and a day late. And so it came of little surprise then, when Pulitzer made him an offer to buy him out, which he accepted, content to make such a profit on what had been a moribund news effort on his part. He would later regret selling out for what would, eventually, be considered to be a small sum, considering the later success of the St. Louis Post-Dispatch.

Pulitzer was developing a new kind of confidence in his own abilities, and manifested this self-assuredness in the creation of a newspaper that would shake the ground of the American reportorial system. Frank White, as a cub reporter, was eyewitness to radical changes right off the bat.

"Mr. Dillon is gone? So soon?" White observed.

"Our paper is not a place for cautious conservatives," Pulitzer informed him.

"Oh?"

"We are going to be having a new man as editor."

Pulitzer craned his neck to address a new visitor to their building.

"Speak of the Devil," he exclaimed. "John!"

John Cockerill was an experienced editor, having done so at the Baltimore Gazette, among other papers, and Pulitzer had made his acquaintance at the Democratic Convention in 1868. Not far out of his prime, in his late thirties, Cockerill was much more physically formidable that his new boss, and cut the air of a true man about town. He was not as cultured a man as Pulitzer, and was more likely to be cheering along at a vaudeville show while Pulitzer was being enthralled by a performance of Shakespeare. His news knowledge was more of the street sense variety, with a basic realism and understanding of the political issues that confronted the man on the street.

"Mr. Cockerill, this is Frank White, one of our up and coming reporters. Frank, John Cockerill."

The two men shook hands.

"Let's get to work," Pulitzer commanded.

Hiring Cockerill was but one of many steps that Pulitzer took in turning the Post-Dispatch into the predominant newspaper of St. Louis. He also hired a business manager as well as other editors to work under Cockerill, for different venues such as arts and entertainment. In the heyday of the newspaper business such organization was common, and it was Pulitzer who first set the template for it.

* * * * * * * *

There was a young man who was briefly employed by Pulitzer in St. Louis at this time who later became quite famous, and a rival of Pulitzer on a national scale.

This young man was William Randolph Hearst, and he worked at the Post-Dispatch as a cub reporter after dropping out of Harvard University. Hearst did not take that august institution very seriously, and was known on campus for a pet alligator that he carried around, giving it champagne to drink. He found other strange ways of being a big man on campus, such as the time he bought up a wagon full of roosters in cages that he deposited in Harvard Yard near the student dormitories at dusk before departing to sleep uptown in the Ritz Carlton so that he wouldn't have to be woken up at the crack of dawn with the ordinary student body. It was from Pulitzer that Hearst learned the basics of sensationalistic newspaper writing, and taking Hearst's demeanor into account, we can see that Pulitzer's seeds fell on fertile ground. Even earlier in Hearst's life there was evidence of his propensity to be outrageous in order to be the center of attention, such as the time, as a child, he smuggled several emergency flares into the bathroom, lit them ablaze and then screamed at his parents through the locked door that he was trapped in a fire. His indulgent father did not even give him a spanking for this transgression.

In St. Louis, it was Hearst's departure that was most notable, though as a reporter the young man had shown a similar propensity to resist supervision from above as did Pulitzer. On this occasion, Pulitzer was hustling into his office with Cockerill close behind him. When Pulitzer deposited himself in the chair at his desk he felt a pop on his backside and immediately stood up.

"What the hell!" he exclaimed.

On the chair was red liquid from a balloon that he had sat on and exploded. To the back of the chair was tied a note.

"It was a balloon, John, with red dyed water in it, and a note on my chair."

"A note?" Cockerill questioned.

"This is the blood of the sheep who read your paper, you old fool," Pulitzer read from the note dryly.

Pulitzer looked at Cockerill, aghast.

"Very strange," Cockerill declared.

"Indeed."

In the hallway they heard the loud bleating of a sheep.

"What on earth is that? A sheep?"

"Couldn't be," Cockerill theorized.

They hustled out into the hallway and looked down the stairs to the entrance, and indeed it was a sheep, baaing in confusion with a note tied around its neck. Cockerill galloped down the stairs to read the note.

"I am one of the idiotic sheep who read your paper, Pulitzer, and it's nice to meet you in person."

"Who on earth could have done this?"

"That Hearst kid, maybe?"

They opened the door and walked out onto the porch, looking about the street. Behind a wooden pole across the street they indeed saw William Randolph Hearst, attempting to spy upon their reaction to his tricks from a secret location. Seeing that he had been discovered as the author of these shenanigans, he blushed like a six-teen-year-old girl, turned on his heel and ran off down the street. He took off for San Francisco, where he used the fortune he had inherited from his mining magnate father to buy his own newspaper.

\* \* \* \* \* \* \* \*

Pulitzer's attacks on the powers that be had thus far been a guerilla campaign. In other words, the scandals were piecemeal, only bits and pieces of the established political machine. Like a classic guerilla military campaign, with full knowledge that the Bourbon Democrats were firmly entrenched, Pulitzer knew that he could not take them on all at once, but chose small battles that he could win. When the machine counter-attacked against him on that front, such as a publicity campaign to contend what a wonderful charitable organization the Black Lantern was, Pulitzer would change tactics, and rob public attention by launching a campaign about bribery in the police force. When the machine tried to shore up the police with a similar defense, Pulitzer would attack the bordellos. The big problem that Pulitzer had was that the machine was supported by the Republican newspaper, which was a much larger and more established source of public information than his rising but comparatively minor paper. The Republican, in a way, was on the take as well, and would help the machine to rebut charges that Pulitzer made against the Bourbon Democrats and the Black Lantern, making Pulitzer seem like a lowly trouble maker who was merely rocking the boat. Pulitzer had to find a way to shake this up.

"If we throw in a fake story that is favorable to the Black Lantern, the Republican will steal it and print it in their own paper, trust me," Pulitzer exhorted.

"Won't they check the facts?" asked White.

"Why should they bother?" his boss corrected. "It's going to be complimentary, and they will feel obligated to carry it."

"They don't want to be late in promoting them," affirmed John Cockerill.

"We can also twist the dagger by giving the story a tweak."

"How so?" White inquired.

"We will write about a party that celebrated the Dark Lantern, and have it be at one of their bordellos."

"That will be rich," chuckled Cockerill.

"They will inadvertently confirm that the Dark Lantern has celebrations at whore houses," said White.

"And we will substantiate the allegation with proof," Cockerill confirmed.

"People are going to find out that their newspaper supports criminals," predicted Pulitzer.

Indeed Pulitzer's forecast came true, and the Republican reprinted the story almost word for word. So, in response, REPUBLICAN STEALS FAKE STORY, blasted the headline in the Post-Dispatch. Also on the front page, a slightly smaller headline proclaimed DARK LANTERN OWNS BORDELLOS, pointing out not only that the Republican thought nothing of reporting that a Dark Lantern party was at a Bordello, but that they did, in point of fact, actually own such an establishment. This edition of the Post-Dispatch certainly changed the level of the political playing field, or so it seemed in the editorial office of the Republican. There, in the office of Jeffery Hyde, a bombshell had exploded. Surveying the dynamic headlines that were broadcast at their expense, Hyde gritted his teeth in exasperation.

"No one checked the facts from this story?" Hyde exclaimed.

"I guess not," Salem sighed.

"You guess not? It was supposed to have taken place in one of their whorehouses and that didn't make you think?!"

"I didn't notice, Mr. Hyde, and even if I had, you know that kind of thing is normal."

"That's not what our readers are going to think."

"We're going to have to be careful."

"He's putting us on the defensive, Goddamn it!" squealed Hyde.

\* \* \* \* \* \* \* \*

Pulitzer's romance with Kate Davis was progressing smoothly, at least smoothly considering Pulitzer's workaholic habits. As his workday was generally from ten o'clock in the morning until the well after midnight, often ended by discussing the events of the day over a cocktail or two, there was little time left for Kate. Women were not allowed in saloons back then, not that Kate was the kind of woman who would attempt to do so. But she was the kind of woman to recognize the limitations that her relationship with Pulitzer would have, and respected him for his dedication to journalism. So, given the limitations, they often met for a rushed lunch in fashionable restaurants downtown, or had dates in the evening on Pulitzer's only free day, Sunday. The first day that he actually touched her was a Sunday, when they watched a matinee performance of Shakespeare's A Midsummer Night's Dream. It was when young ladies dressed as fairies were singing the beautiful lullaby to Tatiana, that the two began to hold hands, looking down from their box above the stage.

Kate actually received the most ardent communication from Pulitzer by mail, for he wrote her lengthy love letters when he was on the road. Occasionally when he took road trips to Washington, oddly, not having his newspaper to contend with, he would have the free time to sit down and write lengthy letters of his feelings and intentions that he did not have the time to do in St. Louis. One day, Kate received the following letter, which said, in part:

"Kate, darling, there is not a moment in my busy day when my heart does not belong to you. I must confess that my brain is most concerned with the politics of helping the little guy, it is true, but it is my love for you that controls my moods, without the emotional relief that I get from you, I will not be able to do my newspaper job properly. Today, in my job, I am researching the stock swindling shenanigans of Jay Gould, and the hope of bringing him down a peg means a great deal to me. But the satisfaction from that pales in comparison to the hopes I have of a romantic dinner with you, my darling, where we can look across the table at each other and share the joys of love. How I wish you were here with me in New York so that we could dine at Delmonico's, and that we can hold true to our engagement and be married in St. Peter's next spring, my darling."

Kate must have been impressed by the sincerity and longing of Pulitzer's words from afar. But she was skeptical considering that he seemed just as far away when he came home, and their personal interactions took up just a fraction of his time. She must have known, deep down, that it was her fate to become a newspaper widow.

\* \* \* \* \* \* \* \*

One evening, Pulitzer and Cockerill strategized over cocktails in a saloon in the late night hours. In such sessions, decompressing from the intensity of having sliced, diced, dissected and displayed the major news stories of the day, they prepared for the battles of the next day's edition by gossiping as comrades, rousing up their confidence at the mighty tasks before them. In the barroom at the beginning of the late night hours, at 1:00 or 2:00 in the morning, when the gas light glow of the late night saloon gave secretive intimacy to their discussion, aided by the affection brought on by a few drinks, they had man to man talks about the gross injustices of the rich and the powerful.

"We are going to throw the Bourbon Democrats out on their proverbial asses," Pulitzer asserted.

"Is the public ready for that?" cautioned Cockerill.

"As we continue to expose their scandals they will be."

"But they still control the purse strings."

Cockerill was far more cautious than Pulitzer, and had doubts about his boss's ability to shake up the powers that be so quickly.

"We're going to straighten that out."

"But that's the problem, Mr. Pulitzer. The people will see us as taking their stuff away."

"Whose stuff? John, you have to realize that in saying that you are falling for their illusion. The stuff is only going to a minority of the population, the Blacksmiths, the politicians, those on the take."

"But those people have a lot of power."

"Unfortunately true, and that is what we've got to change. As we continue to expose their corruption..."

"You Pulitzer!?"

Pulitzer and Cockerill turned around and, to their shock, two large figures stood close upon them. These men were James Broadhead and Colonel Alonzo Slayback, two chieftains of the Black Lantern. They were large, loud, barrel-chested, gregarious men, with the large frame that fit right into an organization of blacksmiths.

"Yes." responded Pulitzer.

"We know who you are!" retorted Slayback.

"And we don't like your attacks on the Dark Lantern, see?!" added Broadhead.

"We're not going to put up with some idiotic immigrant coming into our town-"

Cockerill jumped off of his bar stool to confront the two bullies.

"Your town? Who gave it to you, might I ask!?" he inquired.

"We know quite a few people around here, Cockerill," Broadhead informed him.

"If you're going to act tough, maybe you'd like to step outside, you little weasel," challenged Slayback.

The Saloon was called The Lager Den, and it was a steak, potatoes and liquor establishment, not necessarily in that order. It was also a popular watering hole for newspaper people in the late night hours, and William Hyde and Jeffery Salem of the Republican watched the brutal confrontation from their table in the rear with silent fascination. Fortunately for Pulitzer and Cockerill, who were at a distinct disadvantage size-wise, there was another man in the saloon, Victor Cole, who was foreman of the presses at the Post-Dispatch. He had been having a beer with some other pressroom employees, and hustled forward to come to his bosses' defense when he saw them under attack. His massive size and years of manual labor made him a veritable walking printing press.

"You should pick on somebody your own size!" he blared at the assailants, towering above them.

The two assailants turn around aghast.

"I'll take you on, you bastard!" bellowed Cockerill, trying to save his manly honor.

"You don't have to, Mr. Cockerill. I could mop the floor with these bums," Cole informed him calmly.

He hoisted Broadhead by the belt and back of his collar, like a slab of beef.

"Put me down, you lummox!" Broadhead exclaimed, his feet swinging in the air.

Slayback tried to intervene, but Cole snuffed that effort by using Broadhead like a battering ram to slam him to the ground. The giant printer dragged his helpless squirming captive down the bar and flung him airborne through the swinging doors. Returning to the bar, he glared down at Slayback.

"Unless you want more of the same, get out," Cole declared.

Slayback fled the premises, snarling at what he considered a gross injustice. When he was through the swinging doors, Broadhead screamed a farewell admonition.

"You are not done with us, you two!"

\* \* \* \* \* \* \* \*

Pulitzer's romance with Kate was inching toward marriage, in fits and starts, though Kate did not want to surrender to the possibility of a relationship where she was but a trophy or an afterthought. She wanted more than lengthy love letters from her future husband to prove that she really meant something to him, and tried to secure herself a legitimate bargaining position at least before she was ready to tie the knot. They discussed these problems during a dinner at Antoine's Restaurant, a gourmet Italian establishment, one Sunday evening.

"Sometimes I wonder if you're going to be too busy with the newspaper to make it to the ceremony, Joseph," mused Kate, with some seriousness.

"Kate, darling, how could you think such a thing? Not a moment of the day passes when I don't think about you, wishing I were with you."

"But in person is better than afar, Joseph."

"But I am with you in spirit; you influence me so, darling. I hope I can marry you," said the pleading Pulitzer.

"I don't know if you will have time for it."

"Of course I will."

Their table was in a secluded area of the restaurant, behind a wall of plants where they were protected from other customers. Their waiter, actually the Maître'd of the establishment, had been scrupulous in providing them with privacy. As they sat, however, over coffee and the remains of dessert having this very private conversation, he lurked behind them, clearing his throat.

"Pardon me, Mr. Pulitzer, but there's a most insistent man here to see you. His name is Frank White. We tried to get him to leave, and said you could not be disturbed, but he demands to see you."

"I'm afraid it couldn't be helped. Could you excuse me for a moment, darling?"

Kate nodded with a resigned look on her face, beginning to understand that the juggernaut of Pulitzer's employment was perhaps unassailable.

* * * * * * * *

Pulitzer's political power continued to grow as more readers were lured in by his sensationalistic tactics. He developed a flare for crusades, in which he launched campaigns to assault the powers that be. These had the purpose not only of the object of the crusade, but to increase circulation as readers, being curious of what would happen in a crusade, would follow it as if they were following a soap opera or football team. One of his first crusades was to get rid of the Bourbon's mayor, who, in Pulitzer's opinion, was really a front man who made the decisions that he was told to make. So began a campaign to expose him as a political stooge of the regime, in a daily feature on the activities of Mayor

Overstolz which were comedic in nature, such as Mayor Okays Tax Break for the Wealthy, Mayor Accepts Rail Ticket Price Hike or Mayor Does Nothing. These articles clearly portrayed him as a tool of the Bourbon machine, including one that made fun of Overstolz's name, calling him Understooge.

Increased circulation, as the paper sold 24,000 copies compared to the 4,000 at the time of the merger, brought increased power. With this increase in circulation his support for the Republican candidate, William Ewing, proved more effective. Ewing was a banker that Pulitzer christened an honest businessman, who he portrayed as a far better choice for mayor than the Democratic Party stooge Overstolz. Ewing won the election by 14,000 votes, so Pulitzer had slain his first dragon. In doing so, he was acquiring the power that became like a drug to him. Every day, to Pulitzer, became a day to challenge new villains, and attract more readers. The more readers he could attract, the more villains he could depose, so he worked harder and harder every day to change the world.

William Hyde clutched his temples in frustration in the early hours looking at the spreadsheets of the election results in the early hours after mayoral Election Day.

"I can't believe they got Ewing elected Major," he exclaimed.

"This Pulitzer guy," blasted Salem, "is getting to be a pain in the ass!"

\* \* \* \* \* \* \* \*

After this monumental achievement, Pulitzer found time to get married, and he and Kate knelt down nervously in St. Peter's Episcopal Cathedral, a church that Kate's family belonged as a members of St. Louis' upper crust. The cavernous granite and marble edifice was three quarters full with the social and economic hierarchy of St. Louis, due somewhat to the connections of Kate's family, and somewhat to the professional success of Pulitzer. The place of this marriage, however, in the opinion of his opponents, was significant because Pulitzer's marriage had no connection to Judaism. Though he never became a member of any Episcopal Church, Pulitzer's failure to involve himself with Judaism became a trump card for the anti-Semitics who later attacked him.

Cockerill and White sat in the middle of the Cathedral.

"Look at the numbers on his shoes," White observed, looking at the soles of Pulitzer's feet, which had the number 17 chalked on them.

"Odd looking, isn't it?"

"His shoes are size 17?" White asked incredulously.

"No, Frank, that is the room number of the matrimonial suite."

The suite was not occupied for long, however, as Pulitzer was back in the office on Monday morning, where the struggle with the Dark Lantern was coming to a head. Replacing the mayor was one thing, but dislodging an established political machine was quite another,

"The Republican endorsed James Broadhead for Congress," lamented Pulitzer.

"Waddaya' expect?" Cockerill replied.

"Well, we have to do something about that. He's Jay Gould's lawyer, for god's sake."

If there was a man who people wanted to burn in effigy in the late 1800s, it was Jay Gould. The public despised the short, nerdy looking, black bearded fellow, who was a stock swindler of the highest caliber. Gould grabbed his original financial stake by literally stealing a company from a man who had taken him on as an accountant. Thereafter, Gould became a master at stock manipulation, eventually becoming so powerful that he could almost control the market. He would buy up hordes of a particular stock, as did his "informed" temporary cronies, to raise the price of the stock and then, without warning, sell all of his stock while everyone else, including the supposed cronies, went broke on the exchange. Today the market is much larger, and has different laws to prevent this kind of grand larceny, but in Gould's time he was free to steal in such a fashion and did so. He bought a great number of railroads, principally to inflate the stock prices, and sometimes created a monopoly so his underlings could raise rates without competition, as was happening in St. Louis. For all these greedy deeds Pulitzer attacked him venomously in the Post-Dispatch. Pulitzer and Cockerill were alarmed when Broadhead, one of the bullies who had recently accosted them, and who was both a henchman for the Black Lantern and a toady of Jay Gould, became the machine candidate for Congress.

"Literally a lawyer and a crook," Cockerill grumbled.

"We're going to throw a wrench into their machine, if you'll pardon the pun," Pulitzer announced.

Pulitzer made good on his threat the next day when the headline of the Post-Dispatch queried CROOKS IN CONGRESS?, with a lengthy article about the swindling mechanics of Jay Gould, connecting him for his readers with the Bourbon Democrats, paying particular attention to Broadhead's actions as his lawyer. This article did not stand well with Broadhead and Slayback, who were the featured speakers at a rally that evening, sponsored by the Dark Lantern.

The rally was a classic old style man-bellowing-at-the-crowd affair in a section of St. Louis that was home turf for the Black Lantern. One of their most popular watering holes, the appropriately named Lantern, was nearby, and most the participants had added enthusiasm for the rally because of the libations they had consumed there. Practically in the back yard of this establishment stood a wooden stage illuminated by torches, and the bare ground in front of the stage hosted an unruly but dedicated crowd who were there to root on Broadhead and Slayback, who paced the stage together, ginning the crowd up for supposed revenge against this new crowd of weasels who were becoming their political enemies. Black lanterns and the insignia of the organization graced the wooden fences that bordered the lot, and there were no benches for the burly men to recline upon. This did not bother the lively assembly however, as the brave honchos stood firmly together in manly solidarity with a slap on the back camaraderie that banded them together like brothers. Frank White lurked on the outside of the rally, observing it discreetly for the Post-Dispatch.

As Broadhead finished a speech heralding his mighty candidacy, the crowd invigorated the enclosure with enthusiastic irreverence.

"Don't forget my name and tell your friends, Broadhead for Congress!" he shouted. "Thank you once again, ladies and gentlemen, for your support."

The crowd applauded, cheered, cat-called and stomped their feet.

"Now I'd like to introduce my law partner," he continued, "a Civil War veteran and dashing man who's going to talk a little bit about the nature of our opposition. Ladies and gentlemen, Colonel Alonzo Slayback!"

The crowd erupted again, clapping guffawing, stomping, cheering, hooting.

"Thank you, ladies and gentlemen, your support has been fantastic," exclaimed Slayback, waving his hands before the crowd. "Is he the greatest or what?"

The crowd roared its assent.

"And we know that he'll do a fine job serving the city of St. Louis, do we not?'

Cheers and catcalls verified aggressive and undying loyalty.

"Now I just want to talk a little bit about a certain newspaper that doesn't share our opinion. I should say newspaper, I suppose, it's been called a newspaper, but it's really a scandal sheet, and it's been telling lies about James Broadhead. This so-called newspaper is the St. Louis Post-Dispatch."

Boos and hisses erupted from the crowd.

"This trashy gazette is a really a blackmailing sheet, and has been printing vicious lies about Mr. Broadhead that are completely untrue. The owner of this so-called newspaper is a man named Joseph Pulitzer."

Boos and hisses again

"This is a man who, how shall we say it, is rather new to our country-"

"He's barely off the boat!" blared out a man in the front row.

The crowd laughed.

"Well, that's one way to put it. The fact is that he's hardly a citizen and has the nerve to come to St. Louis and attempt to defame the reputation of a man who for many years has helped to build this town."

The crowd roared their consent.

"So we're not going to let this recently arrived foreigner come in here and run our town, are we?" screamed Slayback.

The crowd erupted with vigorous effusions that they would not.

\* \* \* \* \* \* \* \*

White reported dutifully to Cockerill the next day about the events at the rally.

"Yeah, that's right, he called us a blackmailing sheet."

"What a sleaze ball," said Cockerill.

"And that's not all, then he attacked Mr. Pulitzer as an unpatriotic 'just off the boat' immigrant, who is trying to run the city."

"Well, I hate to spoil the party," scoffed Cockerill, "but, I've got the goods on Slayback."

"Oh?" White inquired.

"I have a quote from someone on the City Council here to put in the paper— 'so far from being a brave man, the colonel, notwithstanding his military title, is a coward.'"

"If that doesn't get his goat," White alleged. "I don't know what will."

"You betcha! Blackmailing sheet..."

Cockerill and White did not realize, perhaps, how much of a risk they were taking in their play to get Slayback's goat. In that time period, duels were a fairly common occurrence, and notions of manly honor were taken very seriously, with such quarrels settled by gun-toting gentlemen. Add this to the fact that Slayback and Broadhead had already attempted to provoke a physical confrontation, and were holding a grudge about the course of that encounter. Such an insult, publicizing the fact that Slayback had been called a coward, was an affront to a "gentleman's" honor, and by the code of honor the "gentleman" must defend his honor or die a noble death in doing so.

The next day Cockerill stood in his office talking to Victor Cole when Broadhead and Slayback came charging up the stairs, with fire in their eyes. When Cole stepped forward Broadhead blasted into him like a football tackle, and it took Cole a minute to wrestle him to the floor. In the meantime Slayback entered Cockerill's office and stormed toward his desk.

"You've messed with the wrong guy this time you little piece of shit! Nobody, I mean nobody, calls me a coward and lives to tell about it!"

Cockerill feared for his life after this threat, and reached into his desk to pull out a derringer and shot Slayback through the mouth, killing him on the spot. A wave of employees flooded the office and Broadhead squirmed through them, astonished to find that his long-time friend lay dead on the floor.

\* \* \* \* \* \* \* \*

The following day, Hyde vowed to make the Republican the lead advocate of kicking that Goddamned Pulitzer out of town. He and Salem brandished copies of the Post-Dispatch while fuming for action.

"They're claiming self-defense, of course, saying they found a gun in the Colonel's hand," Salem exclaimed.

"Which they planted there!" seethed Hyde.

"Cold blooded murder."

During the course of the day the Dark Lantern's organization turned up the heat on the street for revenge, and Pulitzer realized that the shooting would put a road block in the way of his efforts to shake things up in St. Louis, as the whole town, it seemed, was getting riled up. The accused editor, however, was keeping his cool throughout the whole affair. When questioned about it when he was booked in jail after the shooting, Cockerill replied calmly, "It couldn't be helped." He had announced his plea of not guilty (self-defense) as though he were calling an opponent in a game of poker. Yet on the streets of

St. Louis, trouble was brewing, as the Lantern infused crowds boiled with anger outside the Post-Dispatch. In Pulitzer's office Pulitzer and Cockerill peered through a crack in the ominously closed dark green drapes as dusk approached, viewing ruffians on the street below whose strength grew with increasing numbers, illuminated by torches as darkness descended.

"The Dark Lantern's brigades are out," Pulitzer observed.

"Out for blood, perhaps," Cockerill suggested.

Saloons across town were busy as Dark Lantern aficionados infiltrated their depths, and if what was declared in the saloons was true, Pulitzer and Cockerill would both have been dead a thousand times over. Pulitzer had to have police officers posted outside the door of the Post-Dispatch, as the murderous chants of the crowd boiled upward

"Murderers!" they bleated. "Die Pulitzer! Gallows for Cockerill! Revoke the murderers' bail!"

Cockerill and Pulitzer did not feel it would be safe for them to go to the Lager Den that evening.

As the week wore on, circulation of the Republican went up with its self-righteous condemnation of Pulitzer, Cockerill and their allegedly scandalous newspaper, and the sales of the Post-Dispatch went down. Hyde was able to exploit this graphic issue so thoroughly that, thereafter, Pulitzer and Kate became excluded from high society events amongst the upper crust of St. Louis. Life became difficult for the Pulitzers on all fronts. Remember that journalism was not yet considered an honorable profession, so that the wealthy looked down on Pulitzer's problems with distaste, feeling that, having lowered himself down into the depths of common society with his trashy reporting, that he was getting his just desserts.

Kate was flabbergasted at not being invited to the annual Rose Ball that year, an event where she had hoped to introduce her new husband to the world of high society.

"Darling I can't believe it," she pleaded to Pulitzer.

Pulitzer paused, looking deeply into her eyes as he felt her pain that Sunday evening, and did his best to comfort her.

"Kate, I'm sorry, but you must understand that because of my profession there sometimes must be sacrifices."

"Sometimes." she moaned. "Not being invited to the Rose Ball is final and complete."

High society, therefore, snubbed them from the blue blood events that had previously been a fundamental part of Kate's social life, while the lower classes were threatening to lynch them. The combination of these two forces started a movement to pressure the Pulitzers to leave St. Louis without delay, as the irrational pressure of the personal attack blinded the citizens to all of the good things that Pulitzer had done.

\* \* \* \* \* \* \* \*

The pre-trial hearing was much more politically charged than the one Pulitzer had faced previously. The two sides of the courtroom had the same partisan edge, but this time it was far more crowded. Pulitzer's side was now as full as the opposition's, but they were a less venomous group than their adversaries, whose self-righteous indignation reached new levels of intensity in response the assassination of one of their own. The State's Attorney questioned Cockerill on the witness stand, attempting to prove that he had murderous intent.

"So you were out to get Mr. Slayback?" the prosecutor inquired.

"As a journalist, I am not out to get anyone, but simply to report the facts," Cockerill replied.

"Perhaps you'd like to tell us about the facts of the violent encounter you had with the deceased at a bar room just a few nights ago?"

"Oh I'd be happy to. It was Mr. Broadhead and Mr. Slayback who initiated that encounter, Mr. Prosecutor."

"But you left out the fact that it was your hit man who finished it."

"Hit man? Hardly, but that's beside the point. The true assault is on freedom of speech, by people who want to use the power of the government to make money for themselves and their friends. Whose side are you on, Mr. Prosecutor?"

The pre-trial, like Pulitzer's, centered on whether Cockerill had acted in self-defense. Since the government could not prove that the gun in Broadback's hand had been planted, and witnesses alleged that he had told Cockerill he would kill him, the judge ruled that it was self-defense and that Cockerill would not have to stand trial.

The ruling, of course, enflamed the passions of the Bourbons, and their indignation was voiced in the Republican. The newspaper continued to pour on criticism of the Post-Dispatch, contending that their chief editor was a murderer. What could the public expect from a paper which printed scandalous stories regularly on its front page to attract readers? It was no small stretch, therefore, that such barbarians would resort to murder to protect themselves. Pulitzer had to hire body guards to accompany both himself and Cockerill about town, and they continued to be snubbed in high society. This was deeply disturbing to Kate, who had never considered the possibility that her marriage would affect her social standing. It was difficult enough for her to be a newspaper widow, but to suffer exclusion from the social scene she and her family were part of was very difficult for her to bear. Part of this exclusion was based on the fact that Pulitzer's journalistic tactics were breaking new ground for the norms of the day. The upper classes of St. Louis, of which Kate was a member in good standing before she married Pulitzer, did not like sensationalism. They did not see it, as Pulitzer did, as a way to help the poor and underprivileged, but as a greedy way to exploit peoples' lower instincts in order to sell papers. With this incident they enlarged on that theory to contend that the editor of the Post-Dispatch was not only a cheap impresario but also a murderer. As the attacks of the Republican over the allegedly murderous editor continued, Pulitzer realized that he would have to make a

change. After the verdict, accordingly, he called Cockerill into his office for a meeting.

"Thank God they wouldn't indict you."

"Yes, thank God for that," Cockerill responded.

"Unfortunately that hasn't cooled down the
Republican."

"Yes, they're still fanning the flames."

The two men paused, and Cockerill realized as much
as Pulitzer what was coming.

"I am sorry that I am going to have to let you go, John."

"I understand," Cockerill Replied. "Bringing back
Dillon?"

"That's right," his boss affirmed.

"He'll get things back on the straight and narrow."

Cockerill and Pulitzer understood that Dillon,
despite their misgivings about him as an editor, would
calm the waters and get the Post-Dispatch off of its probation with the upper crust of St. Louis. The paper was
on social probation.

"But hopefully, John, your dismissal won't be for
long."

"Oh?"

"I am going to New York to attempt to purchase a
newspaper."

"That's great, Mr. Pulitzer. Which one, if you don't
mind my asking?"

"It's an obscure paper called the World, and owned
by one of our favorite people-"

"Jay Gould."

"I'm afraid so. Hopefully, we won't have to deal with
that skinflint for long."

"Indeed."

"The more major point, John, is that most of the people we've been confronting in St. Louis are pretty small time."

"Not so in New York."

"Much bigger stakes," his boss confirmed.

\* \* \* \* \* \* \* \*

# Chapter 3

# Into the Big Time

The World had changed from being a minor liberal paper to a tool of the robber barons after it was bought by Thomas Scott, owner of the Pennsylvania Railroad, who used it to support his capitalistic railroad ventures. After a time he came to feel that its expenses were more costly than the publicity benefits he received, and sold it to Jay Gould as part of a railroad purchase. Gould went through a similar pattern of use with the little gazette, and through his own propaganda distracted people from his stock swindles and shenanigans. Its cost again outweighed its benefit, Gould came to conclude, and thereafter he put it on the market. He was asking a price far greater than many thought that it was worth, and this was the subject that Gould and Pulitzer dickered over across the mahogany desk in Gould's elegant Manhattan office.

"I must say at the outset, Mr. Pulitzer, that the World is a much better paper than many might suppose, in that it does have an Associated Press franchise, has a long and distinguished history and a very loyal readership."

"Your circulation at present, Mr. Gould, is not even thirty thousand."

"Which is two thousand or so more than The St. Louis Post-Dispatch, so this would be a step up for you."

"True, sir, but as I'm sure you're well aware, St. Louis is a much smaller city than New York as witnessed by The Sun having a current circulation of one hundred and forty thousand."

"True, Mr. Pulitzer, but Charles Dana, as you're well aware, is a professional newspaperman as I am not, and hence—"

"So perhaps, Mr. Gould, you should not be asking professional newspaper prices. Five hundred and fifty thousand dollars is quite a bit to ask, if you don't mind my saying so-"

"Not at all, Mr. Pulitzer, but I must say in return that you'll be getting a fine newspaper building right down next to all the other ones on Newspaper Row and be on your way, from your own point of view, to a fine future-"

"That building I must say, Mr. Gould, with all due respect, is somewhat dilapidated and in great need of repair."

"You've seen the building, Mr. Pulitzer?"

"Indeed I have, Mr. Gould, as well as talking to a few people in the business around town."

"Well you certainly cannot rely on their information, Mr. Pulitzer; they don't want your competition."

"But they do give an honest opinion about your properties. To get to the point, Mr. Gould, if you don't mind my doing so..."

"Not at all, Mr. Pulitzer, go on."

"My offer is substantially less than what you propose."

"Oh?"

"I think a valuation of about three hundred and twenty five thousand would be more appropriate."

"With all due respect, Mr. Pulitzer, I can't bring down the price anywhere near that amount."

"How much could you, pray tell, if you don't mind, Mr. Gould?"

"Well, frankly, Mr. Pulitzer, I wouldn't like to come down at all but I might under duress, as you seem like a fine man."

"Why thank you kindly, Mr. Gould."

"That I might be able to bring the price down ten thousand or so at the most-"

"That, Mr. Gould, I am sorry to say, is completely unacceptable."

"That is most unfortunate."

"Perhaps we can think about it for a day and see if there is some other way to arrange this?"

"Thank you most kindly for coming in then, Mr. Pulitzer."

Pulitzer trudged back to the hotel where Kate was waiting for him, depressed by his encounter with Gould, who he thought was more troublesome in person than he was at a distance. In his heart of hearts, he feared that he could never own a paper in New York City, where he knew lay the future struggles that would change the world. He complained of his plight to Kate.

"And the building is dilapidated, and he wants a fortune for that, too."

"He wants you to buy the building?" Kate asked.

"Yes," groaned Pulitzer.

"Can't you just rent the building?"

Slowly, a grin bloomed upon Pulitzer's face, as he envisioned new, previously unexpected possibilities of achievement, and went back to being his good old dragon-chasing self.

\* \* \* \* \* \* \* \*

Pulitzer returned to Gould's office the next day and proposed to lease the building, and purchase the paper at the ten thousand dollar deduction that Gould had offered, and the terms were accepted. Then Gould proposed a caveat to the sale.

"You would not mind, Mr. Pulitzer, if my son maintains a small interest in the paper, just for old times' sake, his having worked here for a time."

"As long, Mr. Gould, as every day the paper has printed as part of its logo that your family has no influence whatsoever on the content of the paper."

Gould paused for a minute, perplexed, not having expected such a disarming response.

"Very well, pay it no mind."

So Pulitzer departed, after signing the formal agreements, satisfied that his dealings with a man he considered a financial charlatan would be solely economic in nature. Returning to the hotel he broke the news to Kate, who encouraged him cheerfully, despite having the look of resignation on her face he had become used to. Kate was well aware, of course, that her relationship with her husband was opening new areas personally and socially, as she was fleeing with him from the social network of her own family in St. Louis. Could she trust

Pulitzer to elevate her to a respectable position in New York City? Like it or not fate had cast her into that position, so she had to entrust her own future to the ambitions of her husband. Much as she admired his efforts to help the less fortunate she could not help but feel deeply insecure, for her ship was leaving the security of the formal high society of St. Louis into what were uncharted waters. We should note that at this time Kate was six months pregnant, and the thought of going to New York, where she would not have the family connections to help her through the travails of having a child was unsettling to her. Yet, she knew, traditional gal that she was, that Joseph Pulitzer was her husband, and that her fate was cast with his, whatever direction that might be. That evening the couple had what would be their last formal date for some time, and Kate looked across the dinner table fondly at the man she had been so attracted to because of his idealistic ambitions.

The next morning Pulitzer, clad in a formal suit with a stiff collar and black ascot tie, set off to attack his new domain. In the morning he made the rounds of other papers and saloons where he could speak to people privately and conditionally offer them jobs, before setting off to make his premier appearance at his new paper.

The World was an old style paper, and about to undergo a revolutionary change. It was old in the sense that its employees were used to the news being reported in a very sedentary fashion. It was thought, without question, that true gentlemen did not get excited about world events, and they should be reported as just a succession of widgets parading down the ordinary street of existence ah yes, very good sir, and that's that, etcetera, etcetera. Nothing could be further from Pulitzer's intentions and he made it plain in his initial speech upon entering the office. Though a telegram from Gould had preceded Pulitzer's entrance, the gentlemen who sat lethargically waiting for him were probably not prepared for the dramatic and radical change that Pulitzer proposed. As Pulitzer entered, standing erect in his a black cutaway with an ascot tie, his appearance may have given the employees a different vision than the revolutionary statement they were about to receive.

"Gentlemen, you realize that a change has taken place in the World. Heretofore you have all been living in the parlor and taking baths every day. Now I wish you to understand that, in the future, you are all walking down the Bowery. The source of news, gentlemen, is not in the parlor, but in the Bowery, and that is where reporters for the World will go."

William Henry Hulbert, the boss and editor, was the first to react.

"I'm going to resign immediately, Mr. Pulitzer."

"Likewise," intoned another reporter.

"Me as well," followed a third.

All but two reporters trudged out the door with them.

"Well, I'm glad there's someone left to work with. Who are you, sir?"

"James Townsend. I like your approach, Mr. Pulitzer, you're going to liven this joint up."

"Why thank you, Mr. Townsend, the feeling is mutual. And you sir?"

"Albert Litchfield."

"Well?" Pulitzer inquired, prodding him.

"Frankly, Mr. Pulitzer, I'm not in the mood to look for a job at the moment."

"I like your honesty, young man. I think you'll work out well here."

As if on cue, John Cockerill appeared in the doorway of their new establishment.

"John, great to see you," said Pulitzer cheerfully. "Allow me to introduce you to the two remaining reporters from the previous regime."

\* \* \* \* \* \* \*

For Pulitzer and Cockerill the move to New York City was a major league change. St. Louis then had a population of around two hundred and fifty thousand, and New York City was four times that, approaching one million. The massive flow of immigrants through Ellis Island was quickly inflating that mark, and these were the people that Pulitzer would target as the customers to increase his circulation. As an immigrant himself, he was more aware than many Americans of the gross injustices then prevalent in America's inner cities, where people like Andrew Carnegie and John D. Rockefeller ruled the economic roost. In New York City the upper class owned sweatshops, where people worked long hours in very dangerous conditions. These selfish owners made millions and paid no taxes off of the labor of these new American citizens, who lived in desperate conditions in crowded tenements. Pulitzer had many mighty dragons to slay. Municipal politics was rife with scandal, with payoffs to policemen who were well entrenched in their positions as minions of Tammany Hall, one of the first of the mighty urban political machines. Tammany was run by the bribes and favors of new Irish Catholic immigrants, but not exclusively so. (They would protect any immigrant who was willing to join in their scheme of bribery and extortion.) Though Jay Gould led the league in financial chicanery, a cosmopolitan variety of businesspeople did likewise with various and sundry schemes to avoid what little government regulation existed at that time, giving Pulitzer a whole host of scandals to reveal to his readers in order to sell papers.

He had to sell a great number of papers for the debt he was in to Jay Gould was substantial—nearly half a million dollars was a crushing burden of debt. This fueled Pulitzer's ambition, and eventually put a severe strain on his weak constitution. His father, we recall, had died rather young, but this cautionary precedent did not prevent Pulitzer from pushing himself past the brink, despite the advice of some of his close friends not to do so. But Pulitzer was still in his prime when he first entered the ring in New York and it would not be until a few years later that the strain on his health would begin to show.

One of the foremost things on his mind, in 1883, was the election of a Democrat for President, as the country had been electing Republicans for twenty-four years, and there was one Democrat he liked. It was Grover Cleveland, the Governor of New York who embodied, in Pulitzer's estimation, the virtues of the future of the Democratic Party. He was not a crank from out west who spoke only to farmers and miners but a man from the inner city, where, Pulitzer was convinced, would soon be the focus of the most pressing problems that America had to face. If he was going to be of any help to Grover Cleveland, however, as Pulitzer well knew, he had to increase the circulation of the moribund newspaper he had bought, right away, by immediate leaps and bounds.

* * * * * * * *

The following day, Pulitzer and Cockerill took a tour of the Bowery, surveying the arena where they expected to get both news and readers. The streets were crowded with push cart vendors, where an array of nationalities, such as German, Italian, Jewish, Irish and Portuguese, plied their wares. Tall tenement buildings, up to ten stories high, were built within a few feet of each other, so residents of different buildings could have conversations from window to window without raising their voices. Fire escapes were difficult to navigate, as they were packed with wares, some as storage and some as garbage, as regular trash collection was unavailable. The apartments were crowded with recent immigrants, sometimes five or more to a room, who worked in sweatshops, and children might get a modicum of education when quite young before they were sent off, at eleven or twelve years old, to join the workforce

"We should have reporters all over town within the month," he instructed Cockerill, strolling down the busy thoroughfare.

"Where are we going to get them?" Cockerill inquired.

"We'll hire some."

"And who's going to train them?"

"We'll raid the staffs of other papers."

"That won't make you very popular," cautioned Cockerill.

"It's called competition, John," Pulitzer replied stoically.

Their expedition brought them to a clothing factory which employed primarily Jewish workers, who were attempting to hold a strike. The laborers picketed, most of them sporting Orthodox beards and tassels, pacing up in down in front of the building, prohibiting entrance or exit. A posse of policemen had been sent to disband them, and converged upon them, flailing their nightsticks without restraint.

"How many times do we have to tell you that you can't do this without a permit?!" cried out the Sergeant as he cracked a man in the head with his weapon.

The strikers fled in panic, but the retreat of some was cut short by the nightstick injuries inflicted by the police. Six strikers lay unconscious on the dirt packed avenue, while one of their number staggered up to Cockerill and Pulitzer, recognizing them as representatives of a more privileged section of society. He bled from the forehead and limped from a leg injury but was still determined, though he seemed resigned to his lowly economic fate, to cry out for some relief from this gross injustice.

"They vont lettus vorm a union. Tvelve hauer daze vith von hav hauer bleak- klazy-no?" he implored.

Pulitzer had pulled out his small notebook and was grimly scribbling down the atrocities.

"Crazy indeed," he confirmed, writing down the details of one of a score of stories that would crowd the front page of his debut copy of a very enlivened World.

Their jaunt across the island of Manhattan revealed poverty, spousal abuse, drunkenness, unsanitary meat plants, and packs of pickpockets who worked together, in a world that Pulitzer longed to change. Here he saw the millions who came out of Ellis Island expecting to see streets paved with gold, but rather encountered a place where they became the victims of greedy people who would make that gold at their expense. It was Pulitzer who would begin to shake the political ground of America to protest for change for these poor and unfortunate immigrants.

Later in the day Cockerill and Pulitzer observed the nearly completed Brooklyn Bridge which was an architectural wonder of the progress of technology.

"Can you believe that the papers have made this a back page story?" Pulitzer inquired.

"Their loss, our gain,"

"And they ignore the fact that the French have built a Statue of Liberty, and no one has raised the money for a pedestal for it."

"I believe that we have found our first crusade," suggested Cockerill.

"And I believe that people will be thrilled that their names will be listed in the paper for whatever contribution they make, not matter how small."

"Shall we shake hands?" Cockerill inquired.

"Indeed we shall," Pulitzer confirmed.

And so the two comrades shook hands and formalized their first crusade in this new land of dungeons and dragons.

\* \* \* \* \* \* \* \*

The following day, a Tuesday, was an election day, and New York City was having a municipal contest. While Pulitzer stayed back at the World, organizing his new domain, White and Cockerill went out to survey the polling places of the election and were witnesses to Tammany Hall's aggressive methods of making sure that their own machine candidates got into office.

Standing outside of a public school that was converted into a voting place, they watched as a wagon full of quiet but ornery men pulled to a stop in front of the voting entrance. From a buckboard behind it emerged two men who seemed to be coordinating the operation. The first was a thin little fellow in linen slacks and a coarse cotton checked shirt with a straw hat and a pencil behind his ear.

"Come on, let's go, we've got a lot of stops to make quickly, you bozos!" he commanded, in a lethargic monotone.

The other fellow from the buckboard was much larger, a very muscular fellow who dutifully unlocked the gate on the back of the wagon to let the ne'er-do-wells out. He wore overalls over white flannel long johns, and lurked as a rearguard as they trudged toward the voting site. There the smaller fellow seemed to encounter a bit of opposition, as a voting official questioned him about whether these fellows were actual residents in the precinct in which they were about to vote, and a short but heated argument, it appeared from a distance, ensued. The smaller fellow motioned to the larger fellow and, as he approached, he drew his right hand across his neck in a motion to indicate that the poll watcher's head should be cut off. His enforcer promptly pulled out a blackjack and made quick work of this municipal official, and the "voters" promptly stomped down the steps to attend to their civic duty, as the poll watcher lay unconscious upon the pavement.

"Look at that," said White, "the policeman is turning away to ignore the whole thing!"

One of New York's Finest, clad in his dark blue uniform, had chosen to observe the wagon traffic on an adjoining street during this altercation.

"I don't think that this is what turning the other cheek is supposed to mean," Cockerill postulated.

"You don't suppose that he might be under the pay of Tammany, do you?"

"Not a chance."

White and Cockerill followed the caravan to two more stops, where they watched the same process occur with brutal efficiency with minor variations. The second poll watcher acquiesced when he saw the enforcer approaching, and at the third venue there was no opposition whatsoever. It was there White and Cockerill were spotted, and the foreman of the vote packers stormed toward them shamelessly, with his enforcer closely following.

"We don't like being watched or followed, you two," he declared. "Now get your butts outta here before

Claude has to do something about it! Who the hell are you anyway?"

White and Cockerill declined to answer, this being long before the years when reporters were forced to identify themselves when gathering information. They'd seen enough, they concluded, and bounded into their buckboard and snapped the reins sharply to hustle back to the World to report the chicanery they'd just witnessed.

The next day the banner headlines (an inch and a quarter thick, which was new to New York newspapers) declared: TAMMANY PACKS THE VOTE.

Pulitzer had taken on his first New York City dragon.

\* \* \* \* \* \* \* \*

The next day Pulitzer, Cockerill and White sat in Pulitzer's office, organizing their upcoming crusade to fund the pedestal for the Statue of Liberty. Suddenly a brick came flying through the closed window to the left of Pulitzer's desk, blasting broken glass across the room. The brick landed on the floor to Cockerill's left.

"What the hell!" cried White. "Who on earth would do something like that?"

"I think I can take a guess," Pulitzer ventured.

"Tammany would try to strong-arm a newspaper?" White questioned.

"Apparently so," Pulitzer enjoined.

"There's a note on it," Cockerill observed, reaching down to pick up the brick, which had a string tied crossways across the rectangle like the bow of a package, with a crude note tied in where the bow should have been. Cockerill untangled the note, and read it. "If you assholes print any more stories about us packing the vote, things are going to get a lot rougher than this."

"They mean business," said White

"No question about that," Cockerill affirmed.

"We're going to have to show them that we do too," Pulitzer declared.

The next day, Pulitzer sat in the office of the head of Tammany Boss William Henry Tweed, or Boss Tweed, as he was commonly referred to. His office was on the third floor of a white wooden pillared structure with windows that overlooked the fish piers of lower Manhattan where they controlled the longshoremen. He was a rather obese and pockmarked fellow with an air of insolence toward the world, and had the aura of a man who has learned his approach to things from having worked his way up off of the streets. His attire was common, but not shabby, with linen slacks and a pressed white shirt (or boiled shirt, as they called it back then.) A coarse woolen vest was unbuttoned on his midsection, and a half smoked cigar graced the side of his mouth. One of his henchmen stood behind Pulitzer, kowtowing subserviently to the chief.

"We have no idea who threw that-"

"Don't give me that line of bullshit you asshole," Pulitzer barked out. "I'm here to tell you that I will not be intimidated, that the World will not be muzzled."

"Whoa, whoa, hold on there!" Tweed cried out.

"Hold on there what?!" Pulitzer rejoined.

"Aren't we on the same team here? Aren't we both Democrats? Don't we both want Democrats to get elected?"

"True, Mr. Tweed, technically speaking. But I am not your type of Democrat for I am a man of principle, and I want you to know right now that I would support no Democrat who was elected by the fraud you employ."

"Does that mean that you wanted Henry George to be mayor of New York City?" Tweed queried, referring to the radical socialist candidate of the last election.

"Well Hewitt was the better candidate in that race it is true."

"There, you see, it's like I said, we are allies."

"Damn your stars!!" Pulitzer exclaimed. "I am not allied with any man who packs the vote at any time, for any reason."

"Don't worry about that."

"Don't you tell me what to worry about, Mr. Tweed! I'm here to tell you that I will not change my coverage of your organization for any reason, at any time, or in any place!"

Tweed grimaced at his assistant, who reached over and opened the door as Tweed stood up.

"It's been nice meeting you," Tweed volunteered.

"I wish I could say the same," countered Pulitzer, as he rose to storm out of the room.

"He means business," Tweed's aide ventured.

"He doesn't have to be protected from me. He needs to be protected from himself."

Tweed's aide gave him a quizzical look.

"He is going to try to crush the world, and is going to end up crushing himself."

* * * * * * *

The next day Pulitzer, undeterred, strode back out into the melee of New York City, determined to awaken its lesser citizens to incite an uprising against the plight to which they were subjected. He strode though the gang of city folk who amassed in front of a tenement, which recently had been the sight of a flood. Elbowing his way to the front, Pulitzer abruptly questioned an Irish American policeman who separated the crowd from the building's entrance.

"So a four-year-old girl in the basement was drowned by a flash flood from a broken sewage pipe?"

"Ye got it right," replied the policeman wearily.

"How many people live here?"

"I dunno, wadda Iye leuk like, a census taeker? They cram em in like sadeeenes, and dere's nothin' Iye kin deu aboudit. Get on, geddoudahere, stoopid reporder, I ain't a sourzanews."

Determined to find the source of this injustice, Pulitzer had Frank White search the property records to find the owner of this tenement, and accosted him in his office the following day. In a scene similar to his previous encounter with Tweed at Tammany, Pulitzer confronted another kingpin. This fellow's office was more refined that Tweed's, and the landlord, Burton Grimsby, was attired in a black suit and starched collar, though he too, had a henchman, who stood subserviently behind Pulitzer, guarding the door.

"You don't seem to care that a four-year-old girl was killed in your building by a flood of sewage."

The landlord glared at Pulitzer self-righteously.

"I don't own the sewage drains, Mr. Pulitzer, as you should be well aware."

"But it is your building, and I'm sure that you own others like it, with minimal provisions for safety."

"You sure? You'd better do some research on that."

"I already have," said Pulitzer, opening up a folder in his lap, "although the only kind of research any citizen of New York City needs to do is take a walk down any of the major thoroughfares and witness the gross conditions of overcrowded housing in the tenements of you and the other landlords. To be more exact, you own three buildings on Eighth Avenue, six on Ninth and eleven on North, with assorted single and double holdings on an assortment of crossing streets."

"You won't find anything different than you would for the property owners of thousands of other buildings in New York."

"So that makes it okay?!"

"I am not in violation of any laws, Mr. Pulitzer, and if I am, please inform me and I will correct my practices immediately."

Grimsby's attendant opened the door as Grimsby and Pulitzer stood up.

"Mark my words, Grimsby, those laws are going to change."

"Well you let me know when they do."

"In the meantime, we're going to let our readers know all about you!" Pulitzer exclaimed, as he stormed out.

"Nice meeting you," Grimsby uttered tepidly, to which he received no response.

\* \* \* \* \* \* \* \*

One evening Pulitzer and Cockerill decided to do a little night time research, and wandered off into the Bowery in the wee hours to see what was going on. Walking past several saloons reaching the climax of business in the late night hours, they observed one where four rather drunken patrons were being thrown out, rather aggressively, by the bouncers. As they tripped over themselves, backward, falling into the street, a policeman with a nightstick came up behind them and clubbed them from behind in preparation for putting them in the police wagon behind him for arrest. The policeman was a large and muscular fellow with is hair cut close in a flat top, and it seemed, to Pulitzer and Cockerill, that he was used to this kind of work. Suddenly, by complete surprise, the policeman was accosted by the newly appointed Police Commissioner, Theodore Roosevelt.

"So you're the famous Clubber Williams! In case you don't know me I'm Theodore Roosevelt, and I'm now the Police Commissioner. I'm here to inform you that American citizens will not be beaten on my watch. You are now on unpaid suspension pending your termination, Clubber, and will face charges for assault."

Two policeman handcuffed the growling, surly bully, while a lieutenant sat the clubbed individuals on the curb and took information to contact them as witnesses in the upcoming hearings.

"Rosie is not afraid to confront the powers that be," Cockerill observed.

"Unless they are members of the state Republican Party," Pulitzer countered.

Later, when Pulitzer and Cockerill had ridden back to retire at a more civilized drinking establishment, they discussed the character of Theodore Roosevelt.

"Isn't the way he's cracking down on the police going to put him in Tammany's crosshairs?" Cockerill theorized.

"Yes," Pulitzer replied, "but that's not the only boss who will be irritated by him."

"Oh?"

"The Republican Boss Platt gets all kinds of payoffs from the saloon owners to be able to stay open on Sunday. Roosevelt, going by the book, is determined to keep them closed."

Pulitzer was referring to another of the state of New York's bosses, the man who controlled the Republican dominated State House in Albany. Roosevelt had a history of combat with this political machine manager, and fearlessly bucked Platt's efforts to make him cater to the party line. His achievements in the State Capital were few, however, and only in rare cases where he could circumvent the Republican apparatus to force their hand. For this reason he chose not to stay long as an elected man in Albany.

"He's going to have hard time fighting Tammany and Platt," Cockerill suggested.

"Indeed, now he has two powerful enemies to deal with."

"Roosevelt is a hard man to figure out. What is he? Politician, then rancher, now Police Commissioner."

"Don't give him too much credit," Pulitzer suggested. "First he graduates from Harvard and comes down to get elected to the automatic Republican position in Manhattan for the State Legislature. Then he gets tired of Platt shutting him down on his naive reform petitions, so he goes off and blows most of his inheritance trying to raise cattle way too far north in South Dakota, where the cows froze to death. So now he's back here trying to make a name for himself another way."

"You don't think much of him."

"He is a loudmouth and a spoiled brat," Pulitzer concluded.

Pulitzer's low opinion of Roosevelt would lead to a long lasting confrontation that would, eventually, lead to a case before the Supreme Court that would be a signal event in the history of journalism.

\* \* \* \* \* \* \* \*

Pulitzer, Cockerill and White conferred in their morning session in Pulitzer's office.

"Sometimes, gentlemen, making news can bring in as many readers as reporting news," Pulitzer informed them.

"Oh?" queried Cockerill.

"I've got a reporter from Pittsburgh coming in."

"Pittsburgh?" White questioned.

"That's right, Pittsburgh. She is the kind of employee who is not afraid of getting her hands dirty, as they say. Ah, here she is. Gentlemen, allow me to introduce you to Nellie Bly."

Nellie, a determined and plain looking woman, stood in the doorway. As they shook hands, Pulitzer pulled out a copy of Jules Verne's book *Around the World in Eighty Days*, and placed it on his desk. After introductions were made, Pulitzer got straight to the point.

"You are going to go around the world in eighty days, Nellie," he informed her.

"Or less," she replied.

"Preferably."

"Jules Verne doesn't think so."

"Pox on him," stated Cockerill.

"You can check on his opinion when you stop in on him on your way through France."

"He had just a fantasy version," Nellie suggested. "I'm the real thing."

"You certainly are," Pulitzer declared.

For Nellie's departure, Pulitzer displayed a true talent for knowing how to create self-promoting ceremonies to increase circulation. He whipped up public interest with a series of front page extravaganzas outlining her upcoming journey, speculating and predicting the challenges and exotic places she would visit, and readers began to follow her travels before they had even begun. When the day came for Nellie to depart there was a huge crowd at New York Harbor to cheer her onward, and thousands of spectators went wild as she paraded down the walkway in what was to become her classic checkered suit to board the steamer. A brass band played near the ship, alongside a platform full of dignitaries, including Mayor Hewitt, local celebrities and Joseph Pulitzer. As the crowd's cheers rose to a crescendo as the ship pulled out, Pulitzer reached over and broke a bottle of champagne on the ship's hull.

"We have now christened her voyage," Pulitzer cried out to the passionate crowd.

* * * * * * *

# Chapter 4

# **The Competition**

By this time, Kate was raising a baby girl, and was pregnant with another, while being a housewife and newspaperman's widow. The only day Pulitzer was home for quality time was Sunday, which he religiously used as a day to be a father and play with his children. These were some of the happiest times in the home life of the Pulitzers, as he was exhilarated in his new assignment, and they seemed fairly welcome in New York City, with no sign of the social problems they had encountered at the end of their stay in St. Louis. New York City, it seemed to Pulitzer, was larger, more diverse, and therefore more open minded to the new style of journalism he was ginning the town up with, and did not have time for the odd combination of violence and Puritanism that still infected the culture of St. Louis. Pulitzer had grown a beard that concealed the problems he had with his prominent nose and long, narrow chin and he appeared to be a handsome and intelligent man comfortable with being a New York City celebrity. He had purchased a very nice home on 55th Street right next to some of the robber barons he criticized so severely in the World, including the tower-like chimneys that rose above castle-like domicile of one of the Vanderbilt children across the street. The circulation of the World was growing by leaps and bounds, and he was well on the way to paying off his debt to Jay Gould, on whom he did not relent in criticizing in the paper as the financial charlatan that Pulitzer deeply felt him to be.

In this rapid success, however, the first people that Pulitzer agitated were not the robber barons, who expected criticism in the newspapers, albeit that Pulitzer was raising it to a higher level. They were relatively calm, secure in the assurance that their wealth was safe despite the sour grapes of loudmouths in the news business. It was the newspaper owners of New York City who felt much more threatened, and were astonished at how Pulitzer turned a paper they had long ago written off as a moribund non-entity into a living breathing phenomenon that was the talk of the town. Not only was he stealing their readers, which set off major alarm bells, but he was picking up customers who had previously not read newspapers at all, and this made them look bad. Pulitzer was proving, not in words but in deeds, that newspapers should not be information sheets for the well-to-do, but the opposite— revolutionary instruments to raise up the common man against the unfair practices of the rich and powerful. The newspaper owners of New York began to feel like Carl Schurz when he worked with Pulitzer, a step slow and a day late.

The reigning dean of New York Newspapers was then Charles Dana, editor and owner of the Sun. The Sun shines for all, he wrote repeatedly in his paper time and time again, and long had he felt himself to be the real hero of the people of New York City. For years he had exposed the ruthless greed of the robber barons, the bribery and extortion of Tammany Hall and the swash-buckling stock swindles of Jay Gould. Dana had been quite the innovator in his reign, and was the master of subtle sarcasm and indirect accusations. Once he had launched an artificial crusade to praise Boss Tweed, in which he said he would raise money for a statue. For a time people took the drive seriously, and even Tweed himself donated money to the cause. But, as time went on, it became apparent that the crusade was a sham from the outset, and Dana's suggestions of what the plaque on the statue would say, such as "Master of Brib-ery!" and "Organizer of Criminals," it became apparent to Tweed and everyone else that the project was a cha-rade. Dana was the master exposer of the evils of New York. To Pulitzer, however, this was not enough.

"All he does is expose things," Pulitzer lectured Cockerill in a late night conspiratorial barroom chat. "He does nothing to change it. It is as though he wants to keep New York and the rest of the country corrupt so that he can use the issue to sell papers."

Dana had problems with his temperament, prob-lems that sometimes affect humans in their senior years, with particularly noticeable cases if they have been very successful in the public domain. Dana had become somewhat full of himself, arrogant in his abilities and condescending toward his subordinates. In his prime, as a younger man, he would make reporters walk the plank for such egregious offenses as dangling partici-ples, but in his later years his pomposity make him more capricious than a mere grammar master. To people who formerly respected him, especially his employees, he was a man who did not know when to quit (as in retire). By his late sixties, Dana was an ornery, portly fellow, with a long white beard, and his employees trod on eggshells, in fear of being fired for insignificant reasons lest they make the inadvertent mistake of offending the grand sultan's ego.

The three story Sun Building occupied prime space on Park Avenue, and Dana's office had a clear view of New York Harbor. One afternoon Dana sat at his desk perusing a copy of the World while talking to his right hand man, Charlie Moffitt.

"It appears somewhat crass, Charlie," Dana suggested.

"Apparently crass but effective, Mr. Dana."

"The Nellie Bly guessing game, when will she get to Germany?"

"Self-promotional news."

"Bizarre," Dana declared.

"It's the talk of the town, I'm afraid," Moffitt suggested.

"Not in my paper it won't be,"

"Of course not," the subordinate confirmed.

"It's a sad day for America if this kind of charlatan is what the people really want."

"But there is another problem," Moffitt divulged timidly.

"Oh?" his boss inquired.

"Five of our reporters have left to work for him."

"Get out! You must be kidding. When did they leave?"

"They did not return from lunch," Moffitt declared stoically.

"They're leaving my established paper to go write stories for that rag??!! Why on earth would they want to do that?"

"He's doubling their salaries."

Dana turned red, fists clenched, beads of sweat emerging from his enflamed scalp, as, so it seemed, the Gods of journalism had deserted him.

"He'd have to, to get them to write for that scandal sheet."

"Yes sir, Mr. Dana."

"I'm going to find a way to get rid of this troublesome little Jew-boy."

The following day, Pulitzer sat at his desk listening to Cockerill reading the Sun aloud. The article was a front page story with the headline, PULITZER STINKS.

"The slime of his story selection invades the nostrils of his readers like an oily stench. The emotions of those on the gallows, as well as sensationalistic accounts of crime and gossip, litter the front page of the World. In short, dear readers, this so-called newspaper does not seek news but promotes scandals and creates charades to sell papers. To summarize, dear readers, Pulitzer stinks."

"What is making Mr. Dana so mad, I wonder?" Pulitzer queried.

"Probably the reporters we have stolen."

"Maybe."

"We're also about to surpass him in circulation," Cockerill added.

"That might add to it."

"Do you suppose that the Herald is going to join the lynch mob soon?"

"Perhaps," speculated Pulitzer, "but Mr. Bennett is awfully busy partying over in gay Par-ee."

\* \* \* \* \* \* \* \*

James Gordon Bennett, owner of the Herald, was a strange fellow. Having inherited his paper from his father, a penny pincher with Scottish blood, he continued the tradition that his father had started of a paper that covered international issues. As a newsman he was resourceful and innovative, but his personal life often affected the way he covered the news. He lived in Paris because he had disgraced himself at his own engagement party in Westchester County by getting so tipsy that he urinated into, depending on the version one hears, the piano, a closet or a rubber plant. He was, thereafter, ostracized from high society, as his former fiancée's brother attacked him with a horsewhip in Manhattan the next day. Bennett had disgraced a woman of high society, and was expelled from the company of the upper crust. So he moved to France, where he did not have to suffer such social ignominy, and could run the Herald from overseas by telegram.

Aside from his drinking, however, Bennett was an unusual individual, who clearly marched to the beat of a different drummer. He owned a spacious yacht, and often travelled on it around the perimeter of Europe and (infrequently) across the Atlantic. His introduction to sailing had been on a boat owned by his father, and he was on what was the first America's Cup race, which, at that time, was across the Atlantic Ocean. On this race the captain often had to order the young Bennett down into the hold as the headstrong young man was endangering his own life by venturing onto the deck in inclement weather. He sported an impressive Fu-Man-chu mustache, yet forbade any of his male employees from having any facial hair at all. Once, when Bennett scheduled an interview on his yacht for a position at the Herald, an employment candidate with a mustache appeared. Bennett would not let him board the craft, not saying why, and told him to meet him at another location, before sailing off into the mist. When this unfortunate man showed up again with the mustache, he received the same treatment, and journeyed to yet another location, not knowing to shave off his mustache, where Bennett rebuffed him again and sailed away. People felt, with good reason, this news entrepreneur was eccentric and unpredictable. In the news business, Bennett kept the Herald neck and neck with the Sun for the lead in circulation in New York. When he got sick of the high bills for all those telegrams he sent off daily to run the Herald, courtesy of Western Union Telegraph Company then owned by Jay Gould, he protested by laying a trans-Atlantic cable and forming his own tele-graph company, and giving Gould a run for his money. One of his unique ideas for a news story was in send-ing Henry Morton Stanley through the wilds of Africa to find the philanthropic Dr. Livingstone, who lived there providing medical help to the natives. Stanley endured life threatening obstacles in this challenging quest, such as tropical diseases and attacks from the native population, before finding his quarry with that old notable line, "Dr. Livingstone, I presume." When Stanley was feted with a Manhattan ticker tape parade, however, Bennett became incensed. After all it was his idea, the young tyro fumed, why should Stanley get the credit, Goddamnit?!?! As to his drinking habits, one event stands out. He was driving a four-in-hand, a coach pulled by four horses. This was late at night, and he was travelling recklessly, at high speed, attempting to make a grand entry to his home to end his lively evening. The home was actually a castle he owned, but he failed to notice that a stone archway he was about to go through was low. It was so low that when he sped into it the archway slammed into his head and knocked him ass backwards, as they say, off of his coach and onto the ground which, perhaps, sobered him up a bit.

On the same evening when Pulitzer made his observation about Bennett's behavior, Bennett was entering a restaurant in which he was a frequent customer, with his entourage. This was not their first establishment of the evening, as they were making the rounds of drinking emporiums along the Seine. Bennett led the parade down the central aisle of the restaurant, passing by many white clothed tables of this fancy Parisian dining room to a large table in the rear, where he often sat with his sycophants. When Bennett and his laughing and giggling cohorts were about halfway to their destination Bennett stopped, and approached the table of a middle aged American couple, and addressed them in a practiced fashion.

"Good evening. Allow me to introduce myself. My name is James Gordon Bennett, and I am a professional magician. Allow me to show you one of my favorite tricks. Voy-la!!!"

He took a firm grasp on the white tablecloth and attempted to pull it from underneath their dinner with a swift yank. The action appeared unprofessional, and any serious observer would have to estimate that Bennett had no training in magic, for the dinner, including the entrees, sauce boat, bottle and glasses of wine, water, silverware, etc., went flying in various directions, including onto the laps of the diners.

"I am sorry, ladies and gentlemen, but tonight I did not succeed in my favorite trick, but I shall try again tomorrow."

With that announcement Bennett turned on his heel and resumed the march of his snorting and giggling fan club toward their regular table. The couple had stood up, their clothes dripping with the debris of their former repast, as the Maitre'd came scurrying over to the table.

"I'm awfully sorry," he informed them.

"I should say so!" the husband returned..

"Alphonse!" the Maitre'd squealed, looking for his assistant. "Ah, here you are."

The head waiter approached, carrying a tray of towels for the diners.

"We will replace your food and wine, presently, and tonight's dinner will be free of charge. Bring us the receipts for the cleaning bills and Mr. Bennett will pay."

"He's done this before!?" the husband asked, incredulous.

"Yes," sighed the Maitre'd.

"And you allow him back in? You regularly permit this kind of behavior?!"

"He spends quite a bit of money here," the Maitre'd announced ruefully.

Meanwhile Bennett and his entourage arrived at their usual table, where Bennett sat down at the head. As straight up martinis were delivered all around, they made conversation.

"Mr. Bennett," Jacob Chandler inquired, a retired American banker, "have you seen your new competition in New York?"

"Competition!?" Bennett inquired.

"The World, edited by Joseph Pulitzer, and the circulation is up to a hundred thousand, I understand," said Chandler, pulling out a copy of the paper.

"Did I mishear you, Jacob, did you say competition!?"

"Why yes, of course."

"The World, my friends," said Bennett, standing up, "is not competition. The World, I must inform you, is a gutter gazette, a tabloid, a paper for the illiterate, a trash rag, published by Joseph Pulitzer, a Hungarian immigrant who started up a paper in that hick town of St. Louis, where some ignorant ragamuffins fell for his tricks. He will not get away with such delusions in New York. Did Pulitzer send Stanley to find Dr. Livingstone, may I ask?"

His toadies erupted with no's that he did not, while Bennett sat down in a decidedly regal manner.

"His female world traveler visited Jules Verne on her way through town," Chandler pointed out.

"What a scam!" Bennett fumed. "I invent my own stories, and he steals someone else's!"

"Next thing you know he'll be sending her a thousand leagues under the sea," another of their party declared.

"Let's have a look at this rag," Bennett proclaimed, seizing the paper from Chandler. "Well, well, here's a good headline—A Fortune Squandered in Drink!"

This wisecrack brought forth giggles and hoots from his followers.

"Ladies and gentlemen, let me propose a toast! To squandering a fortune on drink!"

Bennett's companions followed their leader's example, and inhaled a healthy gulp of their martinis.

\* \* \* \* \* \* \*

Back in New York, the drive to fund the Statue of Liberty was going gangbusters as another self-promotional news story. A block long line of contributors waited to get in the front door of the World, leading up to a table where Frank White and an assistant wrote down the names of the contributors to be printed in the paper.

"So my name will be in the paper, Mommy?" an eight year old boy queried, holding up the penny he was eager to contribute.

"Ask the gentleman behind the table, Tommy," his mother answered.

"Will it?" Tommy asked.

"Yes it will, young man. Tell me your name now, and let's make sure we get it right."

Pulitzer and Cockerill observed from the landing above.

"This will bring up circulation," Cockerill theorized.

"You don't say," Pulitzer answered.

"People like to be patriotic."

"I guess I'm not just off the boat anymore," Pulitzer speculated.

They laughed.

\* \* \* \* \* \* \*

At his castle in Beaulieu, France, Bennett lounged on his bed in his silk pajamas and smoking jacket, reading through the different American newspapers in the late morning sunshine from the balcony. His secretary, Clarence, stood in the doorway.

"This rag's circulation," said Bennett, referring to the World, "is up to a hundred and twenty thousand?"

"Yes sir, Mr. Bennett," his servant replied.

"He's almost caught us, Goddamnit!"

Bennett fumed, scrunching the paper and looking out the balcony window helplessly.

"There's a way to outflank him," he declared.

The method that he thought was to lower the prices of his paper to compete with the World. The Herald and the Sun papers were three cent papers, whereas the World was merely two cents. So Bennett sent a cable to Dana proposing that they enter a conspiracy to compete with and unseat Pulitzer the newcomer by lowering their prices to be equal to his robbing the mad Hungarian of the main advantage he had over them. Once their superior papers were the same price as his lowly scandal sheet the people would make the right choice and buy the higher quality papers. Bennett and Dana did not recognize, of course, a fundamental problem in their logic: the lower price of Pulitzer's paper was not the only disadvantage that they faced. They failed to understand that the people liked the World because it was easier to read than their comparatively high toned sheets, and that the people would continue to buy it no matter what the competing papers cost.

"I thought that this might happen," Pulitzer revealed, as he and Cockerill strolled Manhattan watching the news boys selling papers late in the week of the new price changes. "How are the sales figures?"

"It hasn't helped them in the least, Mr. Pulitzer. Our sales continue to go up, and theirs stay the same."

"We're going to expand to eight pages, John, and that will fix their little wagon."

It was as though Pulitzer had lapped the competition in a track race, and the main result of the price reduction was to substantially reduce the profits of both Bennett and Dana, as well as and making them both very angry. They failed to understand the much better connection that Pulitzer had with the public imagination, and his success seemed to them to be an undeserved victory. How could it be that this lowly charlatan, this uncultured boob, this Jewish immigrant who used lowbrow techniques to attract readers, could have the upper hand in selling papers? This was a gross injustice, they felt, and the world was going to hell in a handbasket.

One Sunday night, Pulitzer faced evidence of this growing wrath against him. He and his family were having dinner at one of Manhattan's more posh dining rooms, Delmonico's, where they were having a rare family get-together. The Pulitzers sat with Cockerill and White, and were having a fine time with lighthearted conversation. Suddenly Charles Dana approached the table.

"Good evening, Mr. Pulitzer."

"Good evening Mr. Dana, what a surprise. This is Mr. Dana, everybody, owner of the Sun newspaper."

Dana did not acknowledge the introductions.

"I just came to tell you that we know that you're not going to last long here in New York."

Pulitzer raised his eyebrows.

"That's very kind of you, Mr. Dana, but who do you mean by we?"

"The other newspaper owners, who don't report cheap trash."

"You must be disappointed that we are about to pass you in circulation," Pulitzer counseled.

Dana walked away.

"I didn't think they allowed Jews in here, Pulitzer," he said over his shoulder.

Pulitzer's face turned red, and he rose in anger to confront Dana. Cockerill and Kate restrained him from doing so.

"You don't want to give him an excuse to put something else in the paper," Cockerill advised.

\* \* \* \* \* \* \* \*

When it came to choose a watering hole in the crowded island of Manhattan, Pulitzer and Cockerill went off the beaten track. The popular spot for reporters was The Waterson Club, a dignified retreat on Broadway not far from Newspaper Row where reporters could sneak off for a drink at all hours of the day, as some were prone to do. Pulitzer chose Smith's Steakhouse, a smaller bar that was an appendage of a high class steak house that was more of a restaurant than a bar. There he felt he could speak in private without fear of others taking heed of his conversations, and be comfortable with the professional secrecy that had become one of his obsessions. There Pulitzer and Cockerill surveyed a copy of the Herald in the late night hours, plotting a new means of attack upon Bennett and the Herald. They were focused on the lengthy classifieds section in the rear of the paper, which was a major source of income for Bennett.

"How about this one," chortled Cockerill, "beautiful chambermaid for hire to clean men's pipes."

"That's rather suave," said Pulitzer.

"It should say Prostitutes Classifieds."

"Mr. Bennett will be a bit embarrassed when we publicize this."

"Not to mention that it will cost him a pretty penny," said Cockerill, referring to the fact that the charges for classifieds were a significant part of Bennett's income.

The prediction proved correct, as Bennett cringed reading the bombastic headline that declared Herald Helps Prostitutes. Again the smoking-jacketed, silk-pajamad man was having a fit.

"Have them deny it, Clarence. Those ads are personal, how are we to know?'

"Yes sir, Mr. Bennett."

Still smarting from the failure of his price cutting gambit, this defeat rubbed salt in his wounds.

"This Pulitzer guy is really getting to be a real pain in the ass."

\* \* \* \* \* \* \* \*

Pulitzer's first major self-promotional news effort was coming to a grand finale as Nellie Bly was nearing to the end of her journey around the world in eighty days. Readers had followed her travails through the European Continent, into the Nordic Countries and then across Russia on the Trans-Siberian Railroad, into icy Alaska and down through the Canadian Rockies into the United States. Many of the faithful readers of this saga were assembled at Grand Central Station in New York for her return, and again the brass band and local celebrities were on hand to share in the glory, including Joseph Pulitzer who made the big announcement as Nellie reappeared from the train in her checkered suit.

"Seventy two days, six hours and eleven minutes, ladies and gentlemen, we have beaten the challenge of Jules Verne!"

And so the crowd cheered jubilantly as Nellie jaunted back into the real world in New York City, as Pulitzer had arranged for a privately financed ticker tape parade back to the World headquarters. Charles Dana practically foamed at the mouth watching this display of low culture parading down Newspaper Row, and vowed to himself to wreck the career of this insouciant newcomer who was attempting to upset the balance of power in American newspapers.

In the offices of the Evening Post, Pulitzer's former bosses followed their former protégé's progress in his new town. Carl Schurz and Thomas Davidson perused a copy of The World in Schurz's office, overlooking Third Avenue in the uptown building of the Evening Post. The Post was a creation of higher intellectual caliber, as Schurz and Davidson saw it, than the everyday newspaper. They regarded themselves as part of the intellectual elite, who were debating higher order political problems. In politics, as well, they had chosen a different path than Pulitzer, who had departed the Republican Party and had become a progressive Democrat. Schurz was still a Republican, though a dissatisfied one, who did not like the party's selections of candidates that, as he viewed it, favored only the well to do. He was part of a rebel group that argued with the Republicans, supporting candidates for President who did not get the nomination, among other dissatisfactions. They became known as the Mugwumps, who were independent of the general direction of the party, and many bolted and voted Democratic when Grover Cleveland was nominated by the Democrats in 1884. When Pulitzer made his splash in New York, Schurz and Davidson speculated on the crowd pleasing ways that were a far cry from their own more intellectual appeals to the intelligentsia.

"Our boy is making himself known," Schurz theorized.

"He certainly is," Davidson responded.

"Such flashy headlines," said Schurz, pointing to the banner headlines announcing Nellie Bly's return. "He's gotten even more outrageous."

"He knows how to sell papers."

"Look at this, down at the bottom. There is a list of reforms he wants: tax luxuries, tax inheritances, prevent monopolies, tax privileged corporations, recognize labor unions, punish vote buying, my God, Tom, he wants an income tax."

"An income tax?!"

"Yep," said Schurz.

"That will be considered heresy."

"The wealthy will not like that," Schurz theorized.

"No, they will not," affirmed Davidson.

Today, when almost all of these suggestions have become law, it is hard to imagine how radical even suggesting them was in Pulitzer's day. Schurz and Davidson realized that the path that Pulitzer had chosen was far more effective than their own.

"Remember what he told us back in St. Louis?" Schurz inquired.

"Which?" Davidson inquired.

"Preaching to empty pews does nothing."

"His pews are getting fuller by the moment."

"Indeed," Schurz pronounced.

* * * * * * * *

As the high society season of the Upper East Side got into full swing that year, the contradictions of Pulitzer's social status were becoming readily apparent. As a resident of that neighborhood he was a wealthy member of the upper crust, yet his neighbors were the same people he attacked relentlessly, day after day, in the

World. Pulitzer made a regular practice of pointing out that they were paying no taxes on their disproportionate incomes and living in extreme luxury while their employees barely had enough money to survive. He also pointed out the glaring virtual monopolies the robber barons implemented, where they put any lowly upstart who had the courage to compete with them out of business. Despite these virulent attacks, there came a day when Pulitzer's neighbors invited him to one of their social events, at one of the Vanderbilt family estates that was catty corner to the Pulitzer home, so he and Kate had to walk past an array of luxury carriages to make their entrance to this high society event. Seated at one of the many round tables were none other than John D. Rockefeller and Andrew Carnegie, who acted as representatives of the economic powers to question Pulitzer on his journalistic ambitions.

"What is your object, Mr. Pulitzer?" Carnegie questioned him.

"To help the poor people," Pulitzer responded.

"By tearing down the companies who employ them?" Carnegie countered.

"Hardly. My object is to get the wealthy to help the poor."

"We help them with employment, Mr. Pulitzer," Rockefeller argued.

"How do you help them when they are not working, Mr. Rockefeller?"

"Hopefully by giving them a job. The taxes you propose-"

"What about the economic hard times, eh? Were you employing people in the Panic of 1873? Hardly. In times like these it is the duty of the government to intervene."

"Goodness, Mrs. Pulitzer, darling, we haven't heard a word out of you," interjected Mrs. Carnegie, attempting to avert the confrontation. "How do you like New York? Do you miss your family in St. Louis?"

"Yes, Mrs. Carnegie, a little," Kate responded. "But they have been up to visit."

"What about you, Mr. Pulitzer?" Mrs. Rockefeller inquired. "Have you been back to Hungary?"

Pulitzer answered non-verbally with a curt shake of the head.

"Not yet, Mrs. Rockefeller," Kate responded hopefully.

"We have a reporter now you might like to know," Pulitzer interjected, "who is working undercover in a sweat shop in the Bowery."

"Joseph…" said Kate attempting to calm him down,

"You will not be pleased with that little exposé in the paper, I should inform you," Pulitzer concluded.

An eerie silence descended upon the table. This little encounter showed not only the dysfunction of Pulitzer's social acumen but also the problems of his personal demeanor, where he allowed the conflicts of the world to rule his heart, so that his temperament became as volatile as the unpredictable swings in the economy that was ruled by the ruthless robber barons.

The following week the makings of the exposé that Pulitzer had promised were coming about, as Nellie had been employed at a sweat shop clothing factory on the

Lower East Side. This was a fifteen story structure with row after row of knitting machines that rattled with the noise of small locomotives, yet the women who attended them were not equipped with ear plugs. The air was saturated with the tiny bits of cloth that the machines cast off in their gyrations, and entered the lungs of the workers with every passing breath. Almost all of the fire escape doors of the factory had been padlocked to prevent unsolicited breaks, and this hazard would make the factory famous over twenty years later in what was called The Triangle Shirt Waist Factory Fire. Pulitzer was fighting a battle to expose an injustice that was not solved until there was a human tragedy there in the distant future.

Sitting at her machine like the hundreds of other women workers, dressed in a light flowered dress with a kerchief knotted above her brow, Nellie had the nerve to ask for a break. The foreman was incensed.

"You have got to be kidding," he screamed, in order to make himself heard above the din of the machines.

He smacked her sharply on the side of her head.

"You are here to work, young lady, and work you will. Your next break is the twenty minutes you will get for lunch, which you will eat right here. Get back to work!"

* * * * * * * *

In Smith's Steakhouse that evening, Pulitzer and Cockerill, as they liked to do, were surveying the copies of the competition's evening papers, and this night they were reading the Evening Sun.

"Dana is throwing knives at us," Cockerill announced.

"Do tell," replied Pulitzer.

Cockerill began to read.

"Judas Pulitzer is a wandering Jew and a bully, dear readers. He has had to flee St. Louis after his chief editor murdered someone, and has now come to New York to try to play here his same old tricks. The Sun shines for all, ladies and gentlemen, and will not put up with such treachery."

"That's a rather low rent attack," surmised Pulitzer.

"How shall we return fire?"

"I've got an idea on that, John. I've talked to his editor Solomon Carson about coming to our employ, but he doesn't want to be on another team of editors."

"When he's in charge there."

"Right, but, if we put him in charge?"

"And start out our own evening paper."

"Exactly, John."

So the next day, Solomon Carson sat in Pulitzer's office, and found the new proposition much more to his liking, and decided to join Pulitzer's team at a greatly increased salary where he would be in charge of his own paper. Pulitzer counseled him on the task at hand.

"Remember, Solomon, an evening paper is an after-work paper, and the readers are all tired out and don't want weighty issues to think about. That is the job of the morning edition. They want light reading about gossip and scandal to laugh about after work."

"I understand, Mr. Pulitzer," Carson replied.

"A great issue to start with would be that Dana is supposed to be very mean to his domestic help. We have a reporter's account who talked to his help and he sometimes physically abuses them."

"Consider it done, Mr. Pulitzer."

And done it was, two days later, after their inaugural edition, the banner headline read DANA BEATS HIS MAID. In the offices of the Sun, Pulitzer had gotten Dana's goat. The aging editor was beside himself with rage as he read this sensationalistic bombast.

"He's stolen my editor to attack me with this little trash rag!" Dana blared. "In my personal life, Goddamnit!"

"Its circulation is not very big yet, Mr. Dana," Moffitt counseled.

"How big?"

"About 40,000."

"Already???!!!"

"Thirty thousand less than the Evening Sun," Moffitt suggested.

"It's forty thousand too many for a cheap sensationalist!"

"Hopefully it won't last."

"Fortunately," Dana growled. "I've got something now, Charlie. I've got an article from the Hebrew Standard that expresses their resentment that he hasn't the courage to admit that he's a Jew. That will show him up for the coward that he is."

"That'll fix him."

"We're going to chase him out of New York just like they chased him out of St. Louis."

The following evening, in the offices of the World, employees trod on eggshells awaiting Pulitzer's reaction to this vicious broadside. In Cockerill's office, he and White surveyed the headline of the Evening Sun, which said MOVE ON JOSEPH PULITZER.

"Has he seen it yet?" White inquired.

"Yup," Cockerill responded.

But Pulitzer seemed to take this attack in stride, and called the staff together to dictate the next day's lead editorial.

"We appreciate the agonized heart-cry of Mr. Dana, when he lamented, quote 'We wish, Pulitzer, that you had never come' end quote. Nothing could be truer than this. From his innermost soul the broken and humiliated editor of the Sun wishes that the regeneration of the World had never taken place. Unfortunately for him, and the other formerly popular papers of New York, it has. Like it or not, Mr. Dana, the World is here to stay, as a paper for all the people to read, and not just the rich and powerful."

This editorial energized the staff at the World. It seemed like their chief had things totally under control.

\* \* \* \* \* \* \*

# Chapter 5

# Electing a President

"We have got to get a Democrat elected President, God-damnit," Pulitzer growled with conviction to Cockerill and White.

Cockerill sought to lighten up the conversation.

"Mr. Pulitzer, if you don't mind my saying so, you do fly off the handle a bit before elections."

"I am sick and tired of Republican after Republican after Republican as President," Pulitzer droned. "James G. Blaine, another selfish pig businessman with only his own interests at heart."

"I don't think he heard me," Cockerill whispered to White.

"The problem is that the Democrats are stuck in the past," Pulitzer continued. "They still cater to farmers and miners. Can't they see that the future is in the city, where the immigrants are who, I might add, should be their constituency?"

"Grover Cleveland is from the city," White pointed out.

Pulitzer knew that Grover Cleveland was the man he envisioned as the new type of Democratic Party leader. As the successful Governor of New York, Cleveland was an able lawyer and, more importantly to Pulitzer, an honest man. He had nothing in common with Tammany Hall— bribery, extortion, or any of the other urban Democrats that Pulitzer detested, and he envisioned Cleveland as a way to overturn them. Cleveland, however, was not free from personal scandals.

"Whatever Cleveland may be, that out of wedlock child will not help," said Cockerill.

"You're right, damnit," Pulitzer lamented.

Cleveland had admitted to an out of wedlock baby with a woman from Buffalo, but it was not clear if the child was actually his. Despite this he paid the woman to help support the child, (an honest man!) and his political opponents were using this against him. It was late in the summer, post-convention, with Cleveland as the nominee, and the scandal was baring its ugly teeth. In those days, there were no radio or television ads to get candidates' messages across, so they used people to spread the word, and a group of Blaine supporters were organized to march up Columbus Avenue. The mob was marching in lockstep to the tune of their chant, carrying signs that questioned the fidelity of Grover Cleveland.

"Ma, Ma, where's my Pa?
Where's my Pa, Ma?
Where's my Pa?
Gone to the White House, Ha, Ha, Ha!"

Such was not favorable publicity for Grover Cleveland, and Pulitzer desperately exhorted his news team to find some dirt on James G. Blaine to counter this tide of slander that, if left unchecked, would certainly sink the Cleveland candidacy. To Pulitzer, this was political injustice at its worst. There were allegations about a similar injustice in Blaine's own past, with an annulled marriage, including the grave of an alleged baby where the gravestone had its dates chipped off but, like other charges against the Plumed Knight, as he was called, they had never stuck. He had been involved in an insider trading stock deal he had barely weaseled clear of in a Congressional investigation. In that case he'd done a reading of selected supposedly incriminating letters said to prove his innocence, and he again escaped detection by the public. The public was unaware of the Plumed Knight's careful selection of what letters to read, and ignored the fact that he refused to turn over the letters for examination. Pulitzer had his investigative nose to the ground to try to find some evidence to bring that scandal back to life. His passion for elections was especially acute in this contest, and the risk of this weasel Republican extending Republican Party rule for yet another four years made his blood boil.

\* \* \* \* \* \* \* \*

Back at the Sun, Dana's resentment of Pulitzer's success was so deep it affected who he would endorse in the Presidential contest.

"We're not going to endorse the same candidate as that clown," Dana instructed Moffitt from behind his desk, having perused the Pulitzer editorial endorsing Cleveland.

"We can't go with Blaine," Moffitt pointed out.

This was right as rain, as the Sun had a long history of attacking Blaine with Dana's usual relish for sarcasm and invective.

"No."

"Then who are we going to endorse?"

"Ben Butler of the Greenbacker Party."

Moffitt was taken aback by this suggestion, and paused. This was an insane decision, as Butler was viewed across New York City as a crank candidate voted for only by idiotic farmers and miners in the South and West. Surely Mr. Dana did not want to endorse him!? Yet Moffitt was forced to agree for, as usual, the choice was either to agree with Dana or get fired, and he was not fond of the second alternative.

"The farmers like him," Moffitt offered feebly.

"And he's got solid ideas on currency reform," Dana alleged.

"Yes sir, Mr. Dana."

Dana's decision, however, was fateful for this endorsement cost the Sun their readers by the tens of thousands as the campaign moved on. Though high society potentates regarded the World as a trashy gazette of almost criminal tendencies ordinary people were free of this prejudice, and Pulitzer picked up former Sun readers in droves. It made the World able to bypass the Sun and the Herald in circulation, becoming the most popular paper in New York City and the leading paper to support the Democratic Party. Pulitzer was truly leading the charge to give Grover Cleveland New York State and the Presidency.

* * * * * * * *

A few nights later, when Pulitzer sat forlornly after another long night of work, and he felt dissatisfied. He was attacking many small dragons, but the big one, electing a Democratic President he liked, eluded him. The temperamental Hungarian felt like Odysseus stranded on a lonely beach with the challenges of the world floating by and beyond his control. Politics, Pulitzer's primary obsession, was more and more controlling him as the years went on. This contest was acute, with Pulitzer's resentment of all those years of Republican Presidents, and Grover Cleveland, finally a man with the political goals of which Pulitzer approved, truly whetted his political appetite for victory. Besides that his years of hatred for Blaine, the supposed Plumed Knight, who had weaseled his way out of scandals that showed his true nature as a selfish and greedy man, made Pulitzer obsessed with finding ways to drag him down. Therefore, when Cockerill approached him with a finding that might be a way to help do exactly that, it seemed almost too good to be true.

"You might not believe it, Mr. Pulitzer. We have a letter from Blaine asking someone to clear him on charges of bribery."

"I hope this isn't a joke, John. Tell me it's from that old railroad bribery allegation."

"Yes it is, and there's more."

Pulitzer knew of his own over-excited condition and, as Kate and many others were warning him, he made some effort not to aggravate himself needlessly. Yet still the heart pounded relentlessly. Could this be it? The key to killing the greatest dragon of them all?

"Do tell!"

"The first part of the letter is all about bribing the owners of the Little Rock Fort Smith Railroad to not reveal how Blaine watered down his stock— as you know, complicated stuff that we have had a hard time getting the readers to understand."

"Yeah, yeah, yeah," urged Pulitzer, anxious, as always for his subordinate to get to the point.

"But listen to this, down at the bottom of the letter: 'Regard this message as strictly confidential. Do not show it to anyone. Please mail it during the night. Burn this letter'."

Pulitzer could no longer contain himself, bounced to his feet and danced around the room.

"That is something that people can understand!!!"

"We can return fire now, all right!"

So the Hungarian immigrant turned political power-maker launched his now mighty newspaper on the attack against this selfish pig Republican, and soon there were political marchers from the Grover Cleveland side making their presence felt on Columbus Avenue, chanting a different tune.

"James, James, James C. Blaine,

Continental liar from the State of Maine,

Burn this letter!

Blaine, Blaine, James C. Blaine....."

Pulitzer believed, however, there would be further actions needed to provide a victory for Grover Cleveland. The states of the northeast, including New York, had, for the past thirty years, firmly supported Republican candidates. Big business and the cities felt that Republicans protected their interests, and Republican politicians had raised tariffs and promoted the privileges of the large corporations, that, in their view, employed so many people. Blaine was from Maine, and was a local candidate of the northeast. The Democratic Party got its votes in the West and South, where the farmers and miners were deeply suspicious of the banks and the railroads, which were symbols of the Republican base.

Pulitzer felt differently about where the Democrats should get their votes, and worked feverously to arouse the lowly immigrants to vote against these selfish and greedy Republicans, and to vote for Grover Cleveland, who would try to increase the supervision of the government and protect their interests. It drove Pulitzer mad that workers did not see what gross injustices were being foisted upon them by the robber barons via the Republican Party: these men lived upon piles of wealth, paying no taxes on their incomes, while the working man, who made them their great riches, toiled in poverty. So he worked feverishly to find some other publicity to accompany the damning revelation that Blaine was a corporate criminal, and he got it from an unexpected source.

His society reporter, delving into the social goings on about town, found there was to be a fundraiser for Blaine at Delmonico's. Who else could be there, felt Pulitzer, but the richest of the rich. There in the gas lighted early morning hours at the World he mapped out his strategy to Cockerill and White.

"Oh trust me, they'll be there, all the fat cats. Andrew Carnegie, John D. Rockefeller, Jay Gould, John Jacob Astor, Cornelius Vanderbilt and all the rest, throwing money at Blaine to protect their interests."

His eyes glowed with passion and his heart beat with alacrity, he knew that he must seize the moment and plan out the bold coverage of this signature event. A recently hired cartoonist would come in most handy, and the new technology to produce his caricature on the front page would rouse the public imagination. So his plans went forward, and they staked out and reported the dinner as it occurred, and all those slimy, selfish rich characters were there, just as he had suspected, and the cartoon was planned out.

But still Pulitzer was not satisfied, and as he pushed himself relentlessly that night, again burning the midnight oil, determined to leave no stone unturned in order to unearth something that would succeed in cooking Blaine's proverbial goose. Try as he might, he couldn't find a thing, and no new dirt was being unearthed by his reporters. Sitting at his gas-lighted workplace long after midnight, Pulitzer's insides were churning against what he saw as the inevitable chagrin of the election of yet another selfish incompetent Republican President. He had to find something! And so he sat by the telegraph operator of his paper, who surveyed the Associated Press news accounts, which were about the only communications that came in at this late hour, and something came up that he could use. Lo and behold, his prayers were answered. A plant in Maine (the home state of that selfish pig Plumed Knight) was closing and laying off 800 workers. It was perfect. For where was the Plumed Knight while the poor ordinary people of his home state were suffering from terrible economic losses? He was collecting money from the selfish plutocrats who were laying off the people in his home state! (Or at least they were close friends of the people laying them off, but what did that matter?) Here was proof positive he did not care in the least about his own constituents. And so Pulitzer yet again rolled up his sleeves to finish the front page of the next day's edition of the World, which would now broadcast a far more damning portrait of that evil Republican Presidential Candidate.

Pulitzer had a speaking engagement on the waterfront the following evening, where the front page he designed came in handy. Tammany Hall organized the event, with longshoremen and hundreds of other workers in the lively crowd. Many of them carried signs with the front page of the World tacked on to them, and its prominent cartoon of the fat cats throwing money while gorging themselves on Gould Pie and Lobby Pudding. Pulitzer the orator bellowed out his message of self-righteous indignation to the boisterous blue collar malcontents, riling up their anger at the unconscionable cruelty of the privileged class that exploited them so mercilessly.

"At the same time, we should remember, that these capitalist pigs are throwing money into their coffers to elect their dishonest Republican spoils-man from the great state of Maine, something has happened there, Ladies and Gentlemen. A plant has closed in the small town of Lewiston, and 800 people are being thrown out of work. Is Blaine up there trying to stop the plant from closing or to aid the men thrown out of work? Obviously not, we should note. He is too busy collecting money from his ultra-rich friends."

Loud cheers with boos mixed in greeted this observation, as Pulitzer had the crowd in the palm of his hand.

"Why is he collecting this money, we might ask? To help himself get elected is one reason. But why is the rich crowd donating so much money? What is in it for them? So he will help them out when he is in office, make sure that they will keep on paying no taxes, have exorbitant tariffs, which raise the prices for the common man, and not be prosecuted for the payoffs and chicanery that Blaine himself has been engaged in. These are not campaign contributions, ladies and gentlemen, but bribes from the corporate aristocracy to elect a candidate who will keep them in the wealthy and unfair state to which they are accustomed!"

The crowd cheered ecstatically, and some started the Burn this letter chant, loudly trumpeting their indignation. Pulitzer, it seemed, was galvanizing the working class. Would it have a big effect on the election? That was the question. Deep in the crowd, up on platforms to elevate those in the rear, were Carl Schurz, Thomas Davidson and Peter Kepler, all of whom were bemused that this formerly young protégée was now electrifying the crowd like a seasoned speaker. As they were now leading members of the Mugwumps— estranged members of the Republican Party— they supported Cleveland's campaign, and were proud of Pulitzer's efforts.

"Who on earth would have predicted that our boy would storm New York like this," said Davidson.

"He's like you, Thomas," chided Schurz. "He's a heretic who is helping the people."

"A pretty high quality heretic," Kepler observed.

Up on stage, Pulitzer was coming to the crescendo of his presentation.

"Who are we going to vote for?" he cajoled loudly.

"Cleveland!" roared the crowd.

"One more time!?"

"Cleveland!!!!"

Except for the accent, Pulitzer sounded very American.

\* \* \* \* \* \* \*

In the election Pulitzer's dream came true. New York State gave Grover Cleveland the electoral votes to win the election, and he only won the state by a little over a thousand votes. If Pulitzer had not been so relentless in his efforts, James G. Blaine would have been President of the United States. The Hungarian's efforts were there till the last on Election Day, as he was out of the paper to report like a cub from the polling stations, so he could make sure that readers got a full rendition of the excitement of the workers trouping to the polls on Election Day. Then he returned to the World as they awaited the results, and were ecstatic at 5:00 AM when their man was the victor. As Pulitzer put the finishing touches on the front page, the ecstatic headline, CLEVELAND TRIUMPHS! He felt a real sense of accomplishment. He and Cockerill took a walk across southern Manhattan before they returned home, and sat on a bench that looked out at the Brooklyn Bridge, reminiscing about this fateful day. The rays of the sun were just beginning to shine directly upon the bridge, to burn off the nightly fog rising up from the East River. All about them lay the debris of the previous night's last minute campaign, with remnants red, white a blue buntings and streamers of Grover Cleveland.

"They couldn't have done it without you," Cockerill alleged.

"Perhaps not."

"Definitely not."

"Well," mused Pulitzer. "I hope you won't accuse me of being too obsessed with elections again."

Cockerill thought for a moment.

"Depends on the election," he replied.

"How so?"

"Well Mr. Pulitzer, if you don't mind my saying so..."

"Go on."

"Many of us are worried in general about you pushing yourself past the brink."

"Yes, yes, of course, but John, look at what we've done, we've finally elected a Democrat! We've changed the world, I mean I hope we've changed the world, and there's so much to be done."

`"Mr. Pulitzer –'

"Yes John?"

"It's like I said, it depends on the election. You get so excited, spend so much energy, now that's great, but we just don't want you to push yourself too hard. Sometimes we think you should conserve yourself, take a little time off-"

"I certainly couldn't have taken time off during this election!"

"But maybe now you can."

"No John, no. Now that he's elected I have to make sure that he does the things we elected him to do. If not, what was the election for? Workers' rights, unions, income tax, lower tariffs and a million other things."

Cockerill began to think that he was perhaps incapable of getting his boss to slow down. His suggestion in that regard had had the opposite effect. It was as though he had started the gigantic machine of Pulitzer's brain and his will into motion again with but a minor observation, here, sitting on a bench at the crack of dawn after an exhausting day that would have worn out ten men. Joseph Pulitzer, apparently, was caught up in the vortex of the momentum of his own self will, and his friends were incapable of saving him from it.

* * * * * * * *

# Chapter 6

## Crisis

Pulitzer's career forged onward and the circulation of the World continued to grow. Its Sunday edition became the model for other papers, as its pages continued to expand, and provided reading material for what, most often, was the poor man's day off. They read about strange murder cases, exotic locations overseas where new animal species were discovered, or alleged atrocities from the Boer War over in South Africa. Pulitzer also, characteristically, catered to a mélange of immigrant groups. It was the first Sunday paper to be divided into sections, where entertainment, sports, culture and tales from exotic lands all appeared in their own tableaus. The ethnic groups that Pulitzer hoped to save were catered to. Irish Americans received news about resistance to the English occupation; German Americans found out about the nationalistic advances of Otto von Bismarck; Italian Americans were informed about new culinary offerings in northern Italy. In all these ways Pulitzer not only increased his circulation and influence, but also set the standards of the newspaper journalism for the next hundred years. Looking back onto one of the World's Sunday papers from the 1880s shows a creative and interesting paper that made for a fun day of family reading in hundreds of thousands of homes in New York City, and influenced scores of other papers to imitate Pulitzer's methods. The crusade to make Brooklyn part of New York City was wildly popular in that metropolis; Pulitzer continued to fearlessly expose the police bribery and many other scandals involving Tammany Hall; figures of the untaxed incomes of the economic elite were regularly published; the results of real estate records searches exposed the neglectful landlords of the tenements in bold terms. Pulitzer's paper became the champion of the poor, and started to shake the ground for the implementation of many of the reforms that we today take for granted. Perhaps the Progressive Party of Theodore Roosevelt, Taft and Wilson would not have received popular support without Pulitzer, who was truly the man who woke people up to their ability to change their world for the better. Today, looking back, McClure's Magazine is the chief periodical we see mentioned, but it was Joseph Pulitzer who first shook the ground, who raised up the public understanding of the injustices of the era of the Second Industrial Revolution, and demanded reforms such as the income tax long before anyone else.

Pulitzer was recognized for his campaigns by then President Grover Cleveland when the new President unveiled the Statue of Liberty in a patriotic ceremony on Bledsoe Island. Pulitzer sat next to Kate in box seats for the occasion on that sunny spring day in late April of 1884, but gazed resentfully at a section for the fat cats, including Rockefeller, Carnegie and none other than Jay Gould.

"Look at our neighbors, Darling," Pulitzer said to Kate. "They didn't do a thing to help this project, but they sit here nevertheless."

"Go kick them out," she rejoined.

"I'd like to."

When Cleveland gave thanks, however, in his speech before the unveiling, it was Pulitzer's name that was mentioned, as the new President deservedly gave him credit for the outstanding people's campaign that the World engineered to fund the pedestal of the statue. So Pulitzer felt good that day leaving the ceremony, having gotten credit for a job well done. When Cleveland had acknowledged him at the ceremony, however, the President expected some kind of response from the man he considered his newspaper ally, a hand-wave or a bow, or something. Pulitzer did nothing, sitting stone-faced, prompting Cleveland to move on with the ceremony, somewhat surprised.

Pulitzer was nursing a deep resentment toward Cleveland that the President was unaware of, and this resentment would have a deep effect on the President's political fortunes. This grudge was because Pulitzer had been affronted when the President-elect had failed to receive him when he went to recommend two people for appointments in the new Administration. Pulitzer sat in the lobby of the Hay-Adams Hotel with dozens of other men who came to lobby the President-elect. He sat for two hours, his temper rising steadily as he watched many men that came in after him and were summoned upstairs before him, so he approached the two men sitting at the reception table in front of the elevator.

"Gentlemen, I have been here for two hours and many men have come in after me and gone up before me."

"What is your name, please?"

"Joseph Pulitzer!!!"

The man was somewhat taken aback by the explosion, and searched through his paperwork, looking for Pulitzer's name.

"I'm sorry, sir, I don't see you listed, would you like me to put you down?"

Pulitzer stormed out without looking back.

"Goodness me, he's angry," the receptionist declared. "He must think that this is just a neighborhood reception."

A more objective analysis might excuse Cleveland because he had over a thousand such applicants there that day, so Pulitzer's name probably slipped through the cracks via the actions of Cleveland's handlers. But to Pulitzer, the offense was significant and personal. Considering himself a man who had done a great deal to elect Cleveland, Pulitzer was angry that the new President-elect should ignore him, as he seemed to have done that day. The mad Hungarian held onto this grudge, and no longer gave Cleveland the enthusiastic support he had before the election. Over the next four years Pulitzer treated Cleveland indifferently, affecting a dissatisfaction that he did not implement enough reforms during his term as President. When the next election came Pulitzer failed to endorse him or anyone else for President, and another selfish Republican, in Pulitzer's opinion, Benjamin Harrison, was elected President of the United States.

There were other crises, however, that were much closer to home. Pulitzer continued to endure personal attacks from his newspaper competitors, especially Charles Dana and James Gordon Bennett. They continued to view him as a newly minted upstart who threatened not only their papers but the whole institution of respectable journalism. Dana and Bennett never intended to write for the lower classes, and they very much resented that they were being beaten out by a man who did. As time wore on their grudges became deeper and deeper, especially with Dana. Getting on in years, Dana's attacks on the Hungarian rookie were probably hints at oncoming dementia, and were very mean-spirited. Some of this anger was because Pulitzer's success had brought him so much money that he could buy the French Hotel and tear it down- (the same hotel he'd been banned from for being under-dressed for shoe shines during his post-war days of poverty), and erected a twenty story building that was almost seven times as tall as the three story newspaper buildings in the heart of Park Row. Most humiliating to Dana, however, was that it was across the street from his building and would obliterate his view of New York Harbor. He had tried, unsuccessfully, to stop Pulitzer from buying the property, by having the City deed the land for what he termed a much needed park.

At the ceremony to lay the cornerstone Pulitzer was in his glory as a potentate of the news. He sat on the platform with a committee of dignitaries including Mayor Hewitt, as they listened to one of the champion speakers of the day, Chauncey Depew, finishing his introductory oration.

"This building, ladies and gentlemen, is going to be the tallest building in New York City, and the whole rest of the word, by the way, at twenty stories!"

The small crowd applauded gleefully.

"Ladies and gentlemen, Joseph Pulitzer!"

The crowd applauded more enthusiastically as Pulitzer stood up and walked down from the podium to pick up a spade and dig out the ceremonial first shovel-full of dirt.

"Thank you, ladies and gentlemen," he said, bending down to dig up the dirt, and heaved it aloft. "With these new headquarters we are going to be able to change the world!"

The crowd applauded one last time as the small brass band struck up a celebratory tune.

This blatant affront to Dana's power on Newspaper Row was a bitter pill to swallow for the aging newsman. Watching day by day as the girders of Pulitzer's new building rose up to blot out his view of the harbor, Dana became increasingly infuriated by Pulitzer's progress. Pulitzer, a Jew, a foreigner, a sensationalist, was displacing him as the Dean of New York newspapers! He glared out the window of his office instructing Charlie Moffitt:

"We're going to reprint that Hebrew Standard's editorial about Pulitzer's refusal to admit that he's Jewish again."

"That will be for the third time, this week, Mr. Dana."

"We're going to do it three times every week in the morning and evening papers!"

"Okay."

"Don't you see it Charlie, right in front of us, a monument to stupidity! Is this the future of American culture? Are we to sit here and do nothing?!"

"Certainly not, Mr. Dana."

"We're going to start printing it three times every week, until people get the message."

Thus Dana kept up his assault on Pulitzer, but with the blatant anti-Semitism that Pulitzer did not dignify with a response. Along with the brutal religious attacks, Dana continued to add what was his most venomous instruction, in advising his rival to leave New York. "Move on, Pulitzer, move on," he asserted in an editorial, self-righteously insisting this no good dirty Jew and spewer of cheap trash impersonating news should be shunted out of New York City. Dana's readership continued to decline during these assaults, though Pulitzer continued to read every edition of the competitive papers, and was subjected to these bitter attacks regularly. He knew that Dana felt he should be kicked out of New York just as he had been kicked out of St. Louis.

Off in Paris, James Gordon Bennett was also getting perturbed, but for slightly different reasons. In his usual morning at work posture, sitting up on his silk-sheeted bed in his silk pajamas and smoking jacket, perusing the New York papers, Clarence standing in the doorway, Bennett commented on Pulitzer's status in New York.

"This clown is making an impression, you can't deny that."

"They think that he was crucial in electing Grover Cleveland," Clarence replied.

"He organized the halfwits."

"Yes sir. And, I'm sorry to say, there's something a little closer to home."

"Oh?" Bennett queried ominously.

"Arthur Brisbane has left to work for him."

"That buffoon has stolen my managing editor?!"

"I'm afraid so, sir."

Brisbane was an experienced editor that Bennett had stolen from the Tribune, Horace Greeley's old and declining paper. Bennett viewed him as a distinguished and discriminating fellow, and the thought of him working at the World madhouse made him furious. This was an unparalleled cultural decline of unspeakable proportions. It was one thing for this deranged wacko to scrub together a team of lunatics to temporarily (temporary was all that was possible in Bennett's anti-Pulitzer theorem) construct a scandal sheet that would hold the attention of the lower orders for a few months, maybe a year at most. But those creatures of the lower order couldn't really read, could they? That's why they like those coarse headlines about murder and divorce but - Brisbane? Puh-leeze! This was a gross injustice of the highest caliber. They must have drugged him or something.

"Have the yacht brought around, Goddamn it! Tell the crew to prepare for a trip to America. I will do something about this!"

* * * * * * * *

Back at the World, Pulitzer rushed around to prod his reporters onward but, unbeknownst to him, there was new competition in town.

"Where is Townsend?" he demanded, not seeing the man at his desk.

Cockerill and White looked back and forth at each other uncomfortably, neither man eager to break the news.

"Well?!" Pulitzer demanded.

"You haven't heard?" Cockerill queried.

"He's been..." White hesitated.

"Out with it!!"

"William Randolph Hearst has bought the Journal and is hiring reporters."

Pulitzer stood still, in shock, his face turning white, then suddenly scrambled over to the window to look down Newspaper Row to the Journal Building. Lo and behold there was a transformation taking place as wagons full of newspaper equipment, undoubtedly from a train full of same, were being ferried into the building by a team of movers. This was not a pleasant vision for Pulitzer, for this meant real competition of the type that the sedentary papers of New York had not yet provided.

Pulitzer had followed the progress of the young man who had, years ago, we recall, belittled him with a sheep, before returning to California to buy up the San Francisco Chronicle with the money from his father's mining fortune. He had become the Pulitzer of the West Coast, if you will, attacking the rich and famous with bold headlines that clarified the conflicts. He relentlessly attacked the railroad magnates Leland Stanford and Colis P. Huntington as the selfish plutocrats he felt them to be. He also used Pulitzer's self-promotional news stories approach, where the increases of his own circulation were celebrated, in various disguises, as the main event of the day. Pulitzer thought surely that Hearst would stay out west, and that each would tend to their respective geographical areas. Yet here he was.

"They say he did in 'Frisco what we did here," Cockerill ventured timidly.

"He's a goddamn copycat," blurted Pulitzer.

"I wish he would stay in 'Frisco," said White.

"Many wish we had stayed in St. Louis," mused Pulitzer.

But few knew better than he what a real threat this newcomer was going to be.

\* \* \* \* \* \* \* \*

Back on the domestic front, things were not going as well for Kate as she might have liked. Mother of two girls and another on the way, she had her hands full. A governess helped her raise the children and her husband was rarely there but when he was, he exhibited the same dictatorial control he did at his newspaper. This frustrated Kate, who didn't get the quality time with her mate that any wife or husband desires, as she was added with another burden to the many sometimes frustrating challenges of raising children. Unfortunately for her, Pulitzer's demeanor would sink further into inconsiderate and rude dictatorial behavior as the challenges to his newspaper circulation grew with the new competition. That Sunday afternoon her husband had been home and they'd had a fight, all brought on by an innocent joke she had made.

"I'm going to buy a cook stove, Joseph," she had informed him.

"A cook stove! You know how inappropriate that is!!"

"Well I do want to cook better meals for you."

This remark on her part was another bit of sarcasm, for Pulitzer hardly ever ate at home. Her humor, as was often the case, was not detected by her husband.

"It is not your job to cook, God— "he shrieked, then stopped himself, not wanting to use profanity with the children within earshot.

Pulitzer had, like many established men of his time, lived by rather Victorian modes of conduct. In such a lifestyle, a wife took no part in such demeaning chores as cooking or housekeeping. That was what the servants were for.

"Joseph, can't you ever see a joke. I am kidding!"

"Kidding?! I see no humor whatsoever in that."

"Lighten up!"

"I'm leaving. Tom and I are meeting for drinks."

Without as much as a by-your-leave he stood up and walked out.

At the watering hole, now two weeks after Hearst's arrival, Pulitzer was doing his damndest to put a positive spin on things. Davidson was now in his employ, and he paid him much higher sums for book reviews than they were worth. Davidson could not stay on at the Evening Post, where Schurz did not have the kind of financial control he did in St. Louis, and Pulitzer took him on as an act of charity to his former boss. Book reviews, as Pulitzer was well aware, were not a big circulation builder.

"Look at his headlines," Pulitzer declared, surveying the Sunday edition of Hearst's Journal, "they're devoid of substantial meaning. 'Blown Gasket Blasts Boat to the Bottom!'"

"Isn't that what people said about your headlines, Joseph?" Davidson inquired.

He was one of the few people who could call Pulitzer by his first name.

"Sort of, Tom, but it's different. Mine have drama, they have a connection to a greater worldly struggle. They might be showy, to attract attention, but it is for a purpose. With Hearst it seems to be charade for its own sake."

"Most people don't like to think," Davidson said gravely.

"But that's the purpose of a good newspaper, Tom, to make them think. The drama of the front page has to lead them on to higher order thinking, not just giggle at showmanship. Hearst doesn't think about that, he's self-centered, with his own ambitions in mind."

"Think so, Joseph?"

"I know so. He wants to run for President, you know."

"Get out."

"Governor of New York, and then the Presidency."

"With that high squeaky voice?" Davidson asked.

"He's working on that."

"Well, Joseph, I have to tell you, I've got confidence in you, and you still have a head up on the competition."

This remark bucked up Pulitzer's morale.

"Right you are, Thomas, they don't bother me, they're scared," he declared. "They know that our new twenty story building is going to make them seem like small fry."

"I understand that your circulation now leads the pack," Davidson complemented.

"Right-oh, again, Thomas, cheers!"

"To your health and prosperity!"

As they raised their glasses a sudden crash at the entrance turned heads all the way down the bar, where a partially inebriated James Gordon Bennett had just stumbled in, knocking over the podium of the adjoining dining room. He struggled to regain his balance, before lurching down the bar aisle toward Pulitzer.

"I thought I'd find you here, Pulitzer," the mustachioed late night impresario asserted. "I do not like it when people steal my employees, and you are not going to get away with it."

Pulitzer rose from his bar stool and turned to face his accuser.

"And what are you going to do about it?" he queried.

Bennett edged closer to his quarry, but Davidson and other patrons intervened to keep the two antagonists apart.

"First of all, I'm here to tell you I don't like it, Goddamnit! I will not put up with it! I will get you!"

"Get me? That's a hoot. You are just jealous, Mr. Bennett, jealous not only that your employees are choosing to work for me, but that I'm taking your readers, too."

"That's a flat out lie," snarled Bennett.

"Go do some research on the circulation figures," Pulitzer retorted.

"I don't want your readers, Pulitzer. Your paper is a trash gazette for people who can barely read."

"That's another way of saying that you write only for the well-to-do, Mr. Bennett, which means that you won't change anything."

"Change? What the hell are you going to change? Printing gross descriptions of blood, guts, and sex on the front page, and you call that change?"

"You haven't read the right part of the paper, you moron! Read the editorials. What we want to change is the rich living in mansions in Newport, Rhode Island, paying no taxes, while the poor live like animals in tenements working their asses off to make them wealthy. Your paper does nothing to wake people up to the real issues."

The burly bartender came round the bar and seized Bennett from behind, dragging him firmly by the collar and elbow toward the swinging doors, which he prepared to hurl him through. Bennett was not at a loss for words during this forced exit.

"You haven't heard the last of me, Pulitzer, I'm not going to take it, Goddamnit! Don't steal my employees!"

After executing the heave-ho, the barman had the last laugh.

"This isn't the first bar that he's gotten thrown out of," he exclaimed grandly, and the spectators guffawed in support, thinking that Pulitzer had triumphed in the encounter.

The supposed victor smiled in gratitude at their support, and went back to mount his barstool. His old mentor, however, had a keener eye for how Pulitzer felt than the bar room crowd, and saw that Pulitzer's hand was shaking as he went to pick up his drink. Davidson saw that his former protégé was under a lot of pressure, and that the pressure was getting to him.

\* \* \* \* \* \* \*

Back at the Sun, Charles Dana was grateful for the news of the encounter, and pounced on the opportunity to continue his assault on Pulitzer. It is hard to imagine today, when conflict between media personalities are so much more distant and subdued, how personal and visceral the exchanges were back then. Dana's headline was very straightforward and discriminatory: DRUNK FIGHTS JEW, it blasted out on the front page.

"This ought to bring him down a peg," Dana asserted.

"Bennett too, sir," Moffitt responded.

"Who said you can't kill two birds with one stone?"

At the World, Pulitzer's employees, perusing that day's Sun, were curious as to the effect of these assaults on their boss.

"Mr. Pulitzer's not even Jewish, is he? We went to his marriage at St. Peter's."

"Some say that his father was Jewish," Cockerill responded.

"He won't talk about that subject."

"Nope."

"Do you think that this kind of thing is getting to him?" White asked.

"It would probably get to me," Cockerill said pessimistically.

On the following weekend there was to be a celebration at Delmonico's, hosted by the New York Newspaper Association, and Pulitzer would have a chance to socialize with his critics and competitors. It would be in the lap of luxury—the white table clothed dining room with crystal chandeliers, where sommeliers brought forth expensive burgundies and chardonnays to accompany aged beef or fresh Dover sole. Was this an appropriate place for Pulitzer, the champion of the lower classes? What to some might seem as an irony in Pulitzer's character began to appear, for, in his free time, he was not prone to socialize on the Lower East Side with Germans with buckets of beer and Weiner schnitzel, but was a connoisseur of fine restaurants and high class theaters and this night was no exception. He did not shrink from appearing in stride with the other newspaper editors who had long socialized with the upper crust, but his appearance there did nothing to change their opinion of him, for he was still the man who had suddenly, in their opinion, tilted the athletic field on which they played. At the same high class restaurant that Pulitzer had lampooned the robber baron donors to the Blaine campaign event, the high priests of the newspaper world of New York City were toasting their newspaper empires. A few were still resentful of the newcomer Pulitzer's appearance, and unaware of what a big impact William Randolph Hearst would soon have on their domain. There in the bar room/lounge the factions socialized, and newspaper editors clarified their opinions about their feelings toward their competition. James Gordon Bennett and Charles Dana were huddled together in a corner of the lounge, the two most virulent enemies with grudges against the man they considered a callow newcomer.

"I am not a drunk, Goddamnit!" Bennett fumed, referring to Dana's news article about him.

"They say you'd had a few that night," Dana retorted.

"That bastard stole my managing editor."

"He's stolen quite a few from me, the dirty little Jew!"

"That monstrosity that he's building will be the laughing stock of New York City," Bennett quipped.

"How would you know, Mr. Bennett?" queried Dana. "You're in Paris all the time."

"I know a fool when I see one in any town," Bennett rejoined.

"With Hearst here now, there are two fools."

"The blind leading the blind."

"Or the deaf leading the dumb," confirmed Dana.

In another corner of the room Pulitzer and Roosevelt were feeling each other out regarding some articles from the World. Roosevelt, always conscious of the benefits of publicity, wormed his way into the gathering to lobby for better coverage.

"Silk-stockinged commissioner?" Roosevelt inquired.

"We call you that because that's what you started out as and continue to be, Mr. Roosevelt, a silk-stockinged Republican from a rich district."

"You ought to listen to my positions more, Mr. Pulitzer. We have a lot in common politically."

"You are a loyal Republican, Mr. Roosevelt, and you propose whatever will make you politically popular."

"Mr. Pulitzer..."

"We did give you a lot of publicity when you got rid of Clubber Williams."

"Small token there," grunted Roosevelt.

"Well, do you still care about that? I hear you're going to Washington as Assistant Secretary of the Navy."

"Maybe."

"Just don't blow up the country before breakfast," Pulitzer enjoined.

Roosevelt smirked and nodded, surmising this adversary was seemingly unapproachable, and moved on. Pulitzer looked across the room and saw Charles Dana weaving his way to them through the crowd.

"Look out, here comes the lunatic," Pulitzer warned.

"I'll get the net," Cockerill suggested.

"Ah, the Jew who doesn't want to be a Jew," called out Dana to all within earshot.

"Speak of the Devil," quipped Pulitzer.

Dana continued to speak out loudly when he was still on the approach, determined to make a scene whether Pulitzer participated in it or not.

"You're still the wandering Jew, Pulitzer, that's what you are, and you're going to wander out of New York-"

"How so, Mr. Dana? We're building a new head-quarters while you're talking about a new mortgage on your old one."

Pulitzer was pointing out that Dana's lower circulation had forced him to take desperate economic measures, as Dana had to borrow anew on his mortgage to shore up his finances.

"I've taken that mortgage on the building to build a new one, Pulitzer, and to get away from the hideous eyesore that you're putting up."

"You are jealous, Dana," matching his adversaries last name for last name, "of our success while your declining circulation has put you in economic peril."

"Jealous of a Kike? Hardly, Pulitzer. Take that God-awful big nose and get out of town while the wind is at your back you Goddamned Hebrew nuisance.'

Pulitzer lost control and started toward Dana, shaking, but Cockerill restrained him. Moffitt escorted Dana back to his table, but the snowy-bearded buzzard barked back over his shoulder.

"Move on, Pulitzer, move on! You're through here, and we're going to get rid of you as the rabble-rousing scum that you really are."

\* \* \* \* \* \* \* \*

Next day at the paper Pulitzer, as usual, had big plans for his crew. In a meeting to confirm assignments, Pulitzer gave out orders.

Arthur Brisbane was settling in nicely at the World, and Pulitzer had put him in charge of the newly established Washington bureau.

"So, Mr. Brisbane, you're ready to work with those fellows down in Washington and find out where the Union Pacific Railroad is spending that sixty million dollars of public relations money in regard to Congress?"

"Yes sir, Mr. Pulitzer," barked Brisbane, who set off on his way. "I'll get on the 11:15 down at Grand Central."

"Now Cochran," continued Pulitzer, "we're going to change your assignment."

Tom Cochran didn't look the part of a reporter as he was a large burly man but, like Pulitzer, he was not gifted with good eyesight, and had glasses perched upon his pudgy Irish nose. He was one of the reporters that Pulitzer had stolen from the Sun.

"Change?" questioned Cochran incredulously.

"Yes, I'm sorry, something has come up in Albany."

"But I've got tickets to Montreal, and I don't want to go to Albany."

"Don't worry about that, money for the tickets is not an issue."

"It's not the tickets! I have family plans to go to the winter carnival."

"Family plans!! This is a news assignment, Cochran, and the business of the World comes first."

"You can't do that."

"I can and I will, Cochran. If I'd known you were doing family entertainment on a news assignment, I'd have taken you off of it for that."

"You can't tell me what to do with my free time!'

The discussion was getting heated, and both men stood up and faced each other in a pugilistic fashion.

"Free time?!" Pulitzer barked. "Your trip is on World time, not free time."

"You don't own me, Pulitzer!"

Escalation led to a physical confrontation and fists flew between the two opponents, yet only glancing blows were landed before both participants lost their spectacles in the encounter, and ended up feeling for these essential devices on their knees. Other employees intervened to restrain Cochran from further aggression, and Pulitzer left the room in a huff.

Reporters use various methods to unearth stories and, for those about their own industry, gossip sources are often readily at hand. If one were to wager on where the stories in the next day's editions of the other papers came from, conversations in the watering hole (Watersons) would be a good bet. Many reporters did not wait until their edition of the paper to come out to imbibe, and sometimes Pulitzer himself would enter the nearby saloons to check and see if reporters were there rather than out on the news beat as they were supposed to be. The Herald had a front page story on the encounter the following day, and one might assume that the resentful Bennett was gratified that he had finally found a source of revenge, however small, against his hated nemesis. Cockerill read from the story to Pulitzer and White in Pulitzer's office.

"Captain America Pulitzer, clad in his star spangled tights, bouncing from one side to the other of every issue, threw the first blow."

"Bennett has to dig pretty deep for revenge," Pulitzer commented.

"Then Pulitzer received a right cross from his loyal reporter."

Cockerill paused, and hesitated.

"Well, I don't know if we have to read this whole thing, Mr. Pulitzer."

"Go on, John," the chief instructed.

"It's not all that important."

"John...."

"Okay, Mr. Pulitzer," said Cockerill sheepishly. "Which fell right upon his large smeller, which is allergic to pork sausage."

"Okay, John, that's enough."

"Pretty low rent," said White.

"Sticks and stones can break my bones, but names will never hurt me," Pulitzer said, before rising to leave the room, and go about his usual routine of bouncing about the newsroom to supervise everybody in sight. "Come on, come on, let's get to work!"

Cockerill and White looked apprehensively at each other as their boss departed, as they could tell from his body language that the tally from all these emotional attacks was beginning to build up in their effect. They were worried.

One of Pulitzer's most fundamental problems was that he wanted to transfer his own superior talents onto all people who worked for him. This was more difficult in New York, as the staff continued to grow, and he was no longer doing it for merely a few dozen people in St. Louis, but for what came to be hundreds of employees in New York. It was hard for him to be everywhere at once, yet that was what was necessary if he was to be able to impart all of his wisdom to all of his employees. As the World grew this became increasingly frustrating, as stories were written not the way he wanted them, interviews lacking the questions he considered essential, and so on.

It was not only his employees who were worried, however, as Kate was also concerned. Pulitzer had become more and more dictatorial in his home life, and the days of the pleasant father who came home to play with his children were becoming few and far between. His visits to his domicile seemed no longer to be a respite from his hectic work life, but an assault on his family with the same dictatorial vengeance he treated his employees with. Kate invited Thomas Davidson over to discuss this concern, and they sat together having tea in the Pulitzer kitchen, where she tried to paint him a picture of her husband's dilemma.

"He's changing, Tom," she entreated.

"He's got a lot on his plate," Davidson explained.

"But he is different, Tom, and the paper is consuming him."

"Hopefully it will be temporary, and we will relax a little when he's established himself."

"Establish himself?!" Kate lamented. "What does that mean, Tom? Weren't we established in St. Louis? When does it end?"

"He has high ambitions, but a lot of people are out to get him."

"Does it have to be such a personal quest?" pleaded Kate.

What could Davidson do but shrug his shoulders, and Kate had inadvertently pointed out one of her husband's most central psychological problems, his inability to separate the personal from the professional. To Pulitzer, his readers were more like his children than his own family. Losing readers, to Pulitzer, was a personal tragedy, and he felt far more strongly about that than the necessity of being a strong father figure in his own home. As the challenges at the office continued to grow, the coldness to his family increased, and Pulitzer's mood continued to darken. The irony was that Pulitzer was still a very successful journalist, and he was blazing trails for newspapers as no one else had ever done. On the other hand his control freak nature made him increasingly frustrated that he could not exert more influence over the electoral process, which frequently did not please him, as well as being angered at the tension of micromanaging his own newspaper. For as the World grew there was more and more for him to supervise, as he knew strongly that he could do a better job at any position in the paper than any of the people who were doing it, so his supervisory capacities were more and more tested as the paper grew larger and larger. Yet he was still in the hated three story building he leased from that old moneygrubber, Jay Gould. Imagine how this strain might grow when Pulitzer had to move to his new twenty-story building.

The next day at the office, Pulitzer's behavior showed symptoms of the malady that infected him. Rushing about the newsroom, he stopped at the desk of a young cub reporter.

"No, no, no, you can't do it that way, look."

And he proceeded to totally rearrange the young novice's work. Cockerill and White watched from afar.

"The only way it would be right is if the rest of the world were as talented as Mr. Pulitzer," Cockerill suggested.

"He is attempting the impossible," noted White.

Managing the cub at that moment was wearing him out.

"No, no no! How often do I have to tell you this, Goddamnit?!"

Outside their office at that very moment a far more challenging competitor was making a direct assault on Pulitzer's grip on American journalism, for William Randolph Hearst sat on a buckboard outside the front door of the World, on a mission to recruit reporters for his own newspaper. Next to him was the man who might be today remembered at the patron devil of Op-Ed writers, Ambrose Bierce. Bierce's sarcastic and irreverent demeanor gave him the perfect personality portfolio for an editorial writer, as he excelled for years in columns of self-righteous condemnation of the wrong doers in society that the Hearst papers attacked.

Bierce grew up in a small town in Indiana, the son of Bible thumpers, an upbringing he resented for the rest of his earthly days as he would exorbitantly broadcast to any human who cared to listen. He escaped this by joining the only organization he had any firm attachment to his entire life, the Union Army, for whom he fought bravely throughout the Civil War. His bravery was interrupted when a musket ball scraped the side of his head while fighting under William Tecumseh Sherman at the Battle of Lookout Mountain in Tennessee. After the war, to escape the tedium of the Midwestern Bible belt, Bierce fled to San Francisco, where he helped to found an atheistic or at least agnostic utopia, free of Biblical domination. There he wrote columns for a newspaper called the Argonaut, which let him rant about whatever topics about the material world that dissatisfied this spirited citizen, and he also railed his opinions vociferously while imbibing in the saloons that overlooked San Francisco Bay. His columns attracted the attention of the young William Randolph Hearst, when he first formed the staff after buying the Chronicle, and recognized the need for a spirited fellow like Bierce to rouse up the indignation of his readers, and he went to pay a call on this idiosyncratic fellow.

Their meeting is one of the nuggets of newspaper history, as these two unique personalities had their first encounter with each other. Hearst, a tall young man in his early twenties, knocked on the door of Bierce's home and introduced himself as a representative of The San Francisco Chronicle. Hearst's voice was rather high pitched for such a tall man, and made him appear much younger than he was.

"I suppose Hearst sent you," grumbled Bierce.

"I am William Randolph Hearst," Hearst piped out.

And so was born one of the most interesting relationships in American newspaper history. In the famous movie Citizen Kane, Bierce is played by Joseph Cotten, and the portrait is fairly accurate, as Bierce was a sardonic, sarcastic, irreverent fellow, who refused, as a point of principle, to let any man or institution put itself up on a pedestal, and was forever attacking anyone or thing that violated this principle of equality. In the movie, however, it has Hearst firing Bierce, when in real life the opposite was consistently the case. Bierce would get drunk and quit, in a huff, and Hearst would cajole him back to his employ, more often than not by offering him a higher salary. Though Citizen Kane painted a fairly accurate picture of Hearst in some respects, its portrayal of him as a mean and nasty fellow in person was inaccurate. In person, he was the nicest guy you'd ever want to meet; through his papers, however, he could be different. Regarding Ambrose Bierce, he was forever going out of his way to reemploy the bitter and often drunken Op-Ed man, for he realized the importance of retaining this man who fired up his base, as they say, even if it meant what others would consider unreasonable increases in his salary. In this way the seemingly kind-natured Hearst used the far more mean spirited Bierce to do his dirty work.

Getting back to the thread of our story line, Hearst and Bierce sat in the buckboard in front of the World, and one of their lackeys jumped out of the back and walked up to the front door with a speaking cone, opened the door and broadcast up the stairs to the employees.

"Let it be known that we will hire any experienced reporter at the Journal for twice the salary that you are receiving here. One more time, ladies and gentlemen, any experienced reporter from your paper can come to work for us down the street at the newly revived Journal for twice their present salary."

Pulitzer, on hearing this grandiose assault on his premises, was not pleased. It is safe to say that that his blood began to boil as he face turned red and his limbs vibrated as the sounds of Hearst's generous invitation echoed up the stairwell. Then, after a momentary paralysis inflicted by this implosion of anger, Pulitzer dashed down the stairs after the wretched villain, who by then was jogging back to his place in the rear of Hearst's buckboard. Pulitzer raged after him.

"Stay away from my paper you Goddamned charlatan!" he bellowed.

Hearst, unperturbed by this verbal missile, responded over his shoulder as the buckboard jaunted off —

"It's called competition, Mr. Pulitzer."

What could Pulitzer do but languish in despair? Here was a man who had learned his techniques from the master and used them against him with the advantage of a fortune which he had done nothing to obtain. The Gods of newspapers, at the moment, seemed aligned against Joseph Pulitzer.

\* \* \* \* \* \* \*

At their saloon, that evening, Cockerill and Pulitzer bemoaned the new challenges of this brash intruder.

"He did it at all of the papers, Mr. Pulitzer."

"That doesn't make it any easier."

"No."

"I could pay them more to get them back, but what good would that do? He's so crazy he'd probably double their salaries again," Pulitzer theorized.

"He's burning the money from his father's mining fortune."

"Hopefully his mother will shut him off soon."

The following day, however, the assault from Hearst continued unabated. Pulitzer and Hearst viewed the headlines of the Journal, which boldly announced

BROOKLYN JOINS NEW YORK CITY. This was an unprecedented affront for, as they read the tone of the article, Hearst was taking credit for an achievement he had done nothing to attain.

"Now he's stealing our issues, John," Pulitzer lamented.

"Hopefully people will see through it," Cockerill proposed.

"We have long championed the cause of Brooklyn becoming part of New York City, and he's the one having the celebration."

"Yes, with fireworks, Mr. Pulitzer."

"Fireworks?!"

Indeed, Hearst had a flamboyant celebration that marked the kind of explosive sensationalism that was going to be symptomatic of the way he enlarged Pulitzer's methods in a manner which startled Pulitzer as he had once startled other newspapers. Surely, thought Pulitzer, grandiosity this outrageous cannot last, but, unfortunately for Pulitzer, last it did.

In this case Hearst had a brass band far larger than the comparatively miniscule quintets that Pulitzer had employed, but that was far from all of the gigantic spectacle. Remember that Americans in the late 19th century, even New Yorkers, were far from used to seeing fireworks. Beneath the extraordinary exploding fireworks was an ensemble of police on horseback and firemen in their yellow raincoats and bright red hats, standing on their fire wagons, which many New York children had chased through the streets for the thrill of seeing them fight a fire. If this was not enough to amaze both children and adults there were boats from the Navy and Coast Guard in their full colors, with seamen and officers standing at attention in their crisp dress whites. On the platform were a host of dignitaries including Mayor Hewitt and a bunch of lowly Brooklyn politicians next to a slew of grandees of the New York social scene that Hearst had wasted no time ingratiating himself with by buying fancy dinners and other forms of social bribery to make them part of the Hearst propaganda machine. To top it off the dean of New York public speakers Chauncey Depew, who, we might recall, spoke at the groundbreaking ceremony of Pulitzer's new building, was finishing his flamboyant speech grandly denoting the remarkable historical occasion that the whole world should know of.

"And so, ladies and gentlemen, let us celebrate!"

With that final remark Depew gave the signal and the explosive fireworks display began accompanied, no less, by fire hoses pulsating skyward and navy ships tooting their horns relentlessly, as the crowd, churned into a state of gleeful animation, stomped and clapped with wild abandon. Hearst and Bierce, seated in the first row of dignitaries observing the crowd, were quite content.

"Isn't this great, Ambrose?" Hearst queried.

"We practically own this town now, Mr. Hearst," his head lackey confirmed.

\* \* \* \* \* \* \* \*

Back at the Pulitzer home front, husband and wife, unfortunately, were becoming increasingly estranged.

As usual, Pulitzer finished wolfing down his breakfast and was chugging the remnants of his coffee with one leg vaulting outward to spring to his feet and rush out the door.

"Do you always have to be in such a hurry, dear?" Kate pleaded.

"You have no idea what is at stake," her husband retorted stoically.

"Pardon me. Perhaps you could inform me then."

"Hearst is here now, and I have to keep him from beating us in circulation."

"You don't have to play king of the hill, darling."

"If that uncultured slob beats us in circulation -"

"It would not be the end of the world," Kate declared.

"Have you no belief in me?!" Hearst challenged.

Kate's query had assaulted what Pulitzer felt to be central to his purpose in life. How could she change like this? Firm in Pulitzer's memory was that day at the party in Carl Schurz's garden when she had asked him, frankly, what was his purpose in life. Now, however, she seemed to have forgotten, and asked what seemed to him to be uncaring questions. Did she not realize the fatal threat that Hearst presented? Did she not see he was the method without the refinement, the bombast without the key political insight? This, for Pulitzer, might be his greatest challenge in life, for if Hearst succeeded in unseating him in New York City all would have been for naught, for he would be replaced by a cultural boob. How on earth could his own wife not realize this?!

"I certainly do, Joseph! But I don't want you to work yourself to death!"

"That's absurd! I can do the work of ten men, maybe twenty."

"Don't you see, Joseph, that's the problem."

"If I let Hearst win this battle it will be a great loss for the American people."

Pulitzer made his break for the door, having no wish to continue what he regarded as a pointless argument.

"You're putting the world on your shoulders."

"I should," Pulitzer called out over his shoulder. "I own it."

"I don't mean the paper!" Kate rejoined.

\* \* \* \* \* \* \* \*

Pulitzer had an important chore that day, as in a mission to rescue Nellie Bly from another hazardous assignment. Here she had acted crazy enough to become an inmate at the Blackwell Insane Asylum, a place with a reputation for mistreating its residents and, amongst other things, accepting admission for mentally healthy people that their relatives wanted to get rid of. Nellie would be able, during her stay there, to document whether these rumors were true, as she had been there for five days. This was more than enough time, thought Pulitzer, to accomplish the mission's objectives. The asylum sat on a lonely island in the middle of the broad Hudson River just north of the island of Manhattan. It was built of grey blocks of stone erected in the 1840s and perhaps, at least by today's standards, resembled a prison more than an asylum. Pulitzer sat in the office of the Director of the establishment, who appeared to have had his character worn down by years of work in a malignant institution with a long history of foul treatment of its occupants that it would be difficult for any one person to reform.

"The fact of the matter is, Doctor," Pulitzer explained, "that her identity is actually Nellie Bly, and she is one of my reporters. I demand her immediate release."

During this discussion Nellie was in a locked ward on the third floor of the asylum. At that moment she was watching an employee put a lariat around one of the inmate's necks to force him into a cell, where he shoved him onto the floor, released the loop of the lariat and exited quickly while his coworker locked the cell's door. Plates of food partially ignored by the prisoners sat upon the floor and maggots were visible upon them, and an inmate chained to his bed had the temerity to ask for a drink of water and was cuffed by an attendant in response.

In the Director's office, Pulitzer's revelation had roused the Director to a state of smoldering panic. Visions of imminent bureaucratic disaster raced through the beleaguered bureaucrat's head as Pulitzer continued his harangue.

"If you choose not to release her I shall return with a lawyer and a warrant, and we shall add to whatever abuses Nellie has suffered and witnessed the fact that you imprison normal people against their will."

"Wait here, Mr. Pulitzer," the flummoxed man interjected. "I will do my best to get her."

And so Nellie, once back on the mainland, rode back to the World with Pulitzer in the cab of a four- in- hand, while Cockerill had food and drink brought into the World for her to have during her debriefing. Sitting there in Pulitzer's office, wrapped in a blanket, Nellie recounted her adventures while eating hot soup.

"I talked to a forty-some-year-old woman," she recounted, "whose husband had her committed, had their marriage annulled so he could marry a younger woman. They had three children, mind you. Torture and abuse are regular features and the food, so called, is unsanitary and disgusting, to say the least."

"Sometimes I think that the whole world has gone insane," Pulitzer mused.

"So it seems," affirmed Cockerill.

"Life can be very unfair," said Nellie.

\* \* \* \* \* \* \* \*

Despite his success with this story and other campaigns by the World, Pulitzer's chief concern was increasingly the intrusion of William Randolph Hearst into his domain. Hearst's circulation increased with the same kind of geometric bounds as had his own paper at the outset, and Hearst's increases in circulation came, in part, at Pulitzer's expense. In a mere two months Hearst had moved into second place in New York, trailing Pulitzer by a mere ten thousand. The news Pulitzer received from Cockerill the next day was very alarming.

"Hearst has lowered the price of his paper to a penny?!" Pulitzer shouted. "We can't afford that!"

"No sir," sighed Cockerill.

Pulitzer had continued to be the cheapest of the major papers at two cents, with the Herald and Sun having gone back up to three after their ill effected foray into the lower priced gambit. This move by Hearst was infuriating to Pulitzer, who saw it as another money blowing gambit by this brash young whippersnapper who was not afraid to keep blowing his inheritance in a relentless mode of competition.

Pulitzer knew from the statistics that for himself to match Hearst's low balling price would be disastrous financially, and he could not afford, unlike Hearst, to charge less than what it cost him to produce the paper. He also remembered, from his own experience when Bennett and Dana made their ill-advised match of his low price, there was nothing to be gained from it. So Pulitzer felt somewhat incapable of halting the further advances of Hearst into his domain, and became more and more stressed, as time went on.

And so the pressures on Pulitzer continued to build. Always there was the pressure of politics he was perpetually obsessed with. Recently, he had put himself through the wringer about a mere District Attorney race, and the wringer became even tighter when the candidate he favored, who he pictured as a white knight in shining armor compared to his opponent, lost the election. The campaign of anti-Semitism by Dana went on without interruption, which he pretended to rise above but, as an immigrant himself, in his heart of hearts, it ground against him. And the pressure of running the World, in micro-managing now over two hundred workers, so they all would produce work every minute of every day that matched the Pulitzer standards of excellence. Pulitzer was an example of self-will run riot, as the saying goes, as he exhausted himself wrestling with control of everything he came in contact with every day. As time wore on, and various portions of this myriad of things did not go his way he became frustrated and redoubled his efforts to control, increasing the risks of failure and frustration, which attacked him at every turn. With frustration came anger, and he sometimes took this out most often, unfortunately, on his wife, and Kate began to see a side of Pulitzer she had never envisioned when she married him, but came more and more to the fore as his obsessions and frustrations led him, emotionally speaking, into his own self-imposed madhouse.

So, looking for a pair of trousers one morning he screamed at Kate.

"Where the hell are they?!"

"I'm not sure, Joseph," Kate replied.

"Where the hell did you put them, damn it? You knew I needed them today!"

"No, Joseph, I didn't know that. Maybe Miss Smith sent them to the cleaners."

"You didn't know? Well you should have known."

"Joseph –"

"Don't you know anything? Don't you know what my needs are? Don't you know that I had to go to work today and that I have to wear a pair of pants, for God's sake? Didn't you know that?"

"Joseph –"

"Sometimes I don't think that you know anything about running a household, it seems that there's no organization around here. I look now for my pants and you say you don't know, golly gee whiz, maybe Miss Smith took them. That's not much of a help now is it?"

"I don't do anything?!" Kate cried out helplessly. "You have no idea of the lengths I go to for you around here."

But Kate could not continue her plea, and she broke out in tears and left the room.

Pulitzer was so enmeshed in his worldly struggles that he did not do what a conscientious husband should have done, apologize, set things right, exercise some compassion toward his wife to make up for his own misbehavior. Unfortunately he regarded himself in the right, put on some inferior trousers and stormed out the door to go to work. Thereafter, at work, he continued in his usual habits of dictatorial control on all the actions of his subordinates.

"Let's go, you blockheads, let's get these editorials in here. Time's a wasting! I haven't got all day."

White and Cockerill hustled into Pulitzer's office, and placed their writings on his desk.

"Thank you, gentlemen," Pulitzer announced, and attempted to begin the job of his own brutal editing and redirection that his employees were so used to.

Pulitzer's physical constitution, however, had been pushed past the brink. Remember that, even as a brilliant man he had a very weak constitution. He was tall, very skinny, wearing thick spectacles because of his poor vision. He was caught in his own trap of fate as the excessive Napoleonic ambition of his own self-will which inflicted stress that his delicate physical frame did not have the capacity to endure. So, that day, the awful hand of time caught up with him, and he encountered its merciless consequences. Try as he might, putting the papers at varying lengths from his eyes, Pulitzer could not read their contents at any distance. Then, as he looked up, his vision, he discovered, had retreated further, for even the physical features of Cockerill and White had become blurry features on what had become a murky horizon. He was losing his vision, but this must be temporary it would come back, surely. How could it be otherwise? He had so much to do! Why he was a young and healthy man, forty-one years old, was he not? Pulitzer sprang up to his feet.

"God damn it! I can't read. Could you please get me a carriage, gentlemen? I'm going home for the day."

"Right away, Mr. Pulitzer," Cockerill replied, as White jogged off to the back of the building.

"Well, I've trained you all quite well, I hope, so you'll be able to see to your duties in my absence that, I assure you, will be only temporary."

Pulitzer attempted to strut boldly toward the door of his office but did not see the dull image of the waste can at his feet and tripped over it, and Cockerill reached down and snatched it out of the way. He attempted to guide Pulitzer by the arm down the hallway but his boss adamantly refused, and pulled his elbow viciously away.

"I can make it down the stairs, God damn it!"

He stomped down the hallway and felt his way to the edge of the stairway, but then tripped down the first few stairs when he missed his grip on the hand rail.

"Mr. Pulitzer," pleaded Cockerill, approaching from behind.

But Pulitzer's strong will was completely unaffected by mere physical frailties.

"Leave me alone!" he commanded, and grasped the rail strongly as he propelled himself down the stairs with grim determination.

Shoving his way through the doorway he felt his way up to his seat on the coach next to Victor Cole, shaking off the help of White as he had of Cockerill. Cole silently snapped the reins, and the buckboard departed.

\* \* \* \* \* \* \* \*

# Chapter 7

## A New Way of Life

This medical disaster would make the rest of Pulitzer's life, unfortunately, very difficult, as one of his eyes had a broken blood vessel, with major damage to the other. He became legally blind, but this was not all of the problem. His frail constitution had deteriorated in other ways, including asthma, weak lungs, stomach problems and worsened bouts of depression made more intense by the frustrations brought on by the debilitation of blindness. The anger and anguish that wracked his frame were so intense that he became a nervous wreck, wherein the slightest of noises, such as the striking of a match, would be enough to push him off an emotional cliff. In this condition the psychological problems that had previously plagued him to various degrees became far worse, and he became more likely to vent his anger upon those about him without thinking of the consequences. For a man as talented as Pulitzer, who was multi-lingual with a prodigious memory, with excellent writing abilities, and organizational skills that few could match, to mention a few of his talents, life would be a lonely enterprise, for his contact with the outside world had become seriously impaired. Pulitzer, like all true geniuses, had far more curiosity than a normal human being, and a relentlessly strong will to satisfy that curiosity. Hence the condition that fate thrust him into was one of the cruelest that Mother Nature could have chosen, for how was he to satisfy that curiosity without the gift of sight? Deprived of the ability to take in information he would become bored and, as the saying goes, an idle mind is the devil's workshop, so Pulitzer would be the victim of serious bouts of depression. On top of all that he was a workaholic, and his mania to get things done is what had prevented him from following the advice of friends and colleagues to not push himself past the brink. After his breakdown he acknowledged the truth of the previous suggestions but it was far too late. At the very beginning of this new physical and mental confinement the doctors gave suggestions that made Pulitzer angry, for they felt he should cease to engage in the ambitious work activities he was so addicted to.

Two physicians came to give their diagnoses on the day he was brought home, Dr. Herman Knapp, Manhattan's best eye doctor, accompanied family physician, Dr. McLane. Dr. Knapp, following the preliminary examination, was advising Pulitzer on his physical condition and providing recommendations for his recovery, while Dr. McLane came out to see Kate, who had waited nervously outside their bedroom.

"How bad is it?" Kate inquired.

"Dr. Knapp could give you a better description than me, Mrs. Pulitzer," McLane informed her, "as he is an eye specialist, but I am afraid that Mr. Pulitzer has lost most all of his vision."

"Permanently?"

"That depends on how well Mr. Pulitzer follows directions."

"Directions?" Kate asked suspiciously.

"Dr. Knapp is advising Mr. Pulitzer to start out by staying in a dark room for six weeks to rest his eyes and stop the damage to the blood vessels. Thereafter, to continue to allow his body to regain its strength, he should retire from professional work so that, in time, hopefully, his physical constitution will recover."

"You want him to quit the newspaper business?"

"I am afraid so," McLane remarked, "and we feel that rest and peace of mind are going to have to be a very important part of his recovery process."

"Telling him to stop working is not going to get a peaceful reception, Dr. McLane."

"Maybe not right away, but that's where we need your help. Surely he's made enough money for a thousand men to retire with, and the two of you can go off and live the life of leisure that's dreamed of by millions."

"It's not dreamed of by Joseph Pulitzer, I'm afraid."

As if on cue, Pulitzer's powerful voice could be heard blasting through the bedroom door.

"Six weeks of doing nothing sitting in a dark room and then retirement?! You might as well send me to the hangman!!!"

The orders of the doctors were literally the last possible thing he wanted to hear. His newspapers were like parts of his physical and emotional being, and asking him to quit working with them was like asking him to cut off an arm or a leg. Increasing the circulation of his newspapers was, to him, like breathing air, the very reason for his existence. What the doctors said to him was unimaginably bad, and as much as Kate might try to comfort him under the circumstances, his mood darkened so he became a man difficult for anyone to assist. Strong-willed man he was, he plotted and planned how to overcome these great obstacles and resume, to the best of his ability, the life he'd had before his breakdown.

\* \* \* \* \* \* \* \*

Kate was in a difficult position as, relatively new to New York, separated from her family in St. Louis, and very busy raising three children, she did not have many friends to reach out to. Thomas Davidson was the one long lasting friend she knew in town, and invited him over to discuss her husband's difficulties.

"The doctors want him to retire from the newspaper business," she confided.

"He is not going to like that," stated Davidson.

"And I don't know what kind of help that I can be, but the doctors want me to try."

"It will be hard at first, but he will find a way."

"A way to what?" Kate inquired.

"To run his newspapers."

"In his condition?"

"Kate, you know that your husband is a very strong-willed man, and he is not going to let a couple of doctors deter him."

"But his doctors say that he's at his wits end."

"Yes, he's been pushing himself past the brink," said Davidson ruefully.

"And now it's too late to go back."

Tears came to Kate's eyes.

"But Kate, you know that his beliefs are strong, and he's going to try to accomplish them no matter what the obstacles are."

"Is that good or bad? He might frustrate himself and worsen his condition. At least that's what the doctors say."

"Your husband is going to be himself, Kate."

"Himself," mused Kate.

"There's some good news," Davidson stated.

"Oh?"

"Hearst has raised the price of his paper back to two cents."

"Sounds like a consolation prize."

Overcoming the obstacles, finding a way, working hard no matter what—there was the problem. It was Pulitzer's addiction to work, to solving the world's problems, to slaying all of those merciless dragons that assaulted the common citizen, and he had, in his own estimation, only just begun to accomplish some of his objectives. For the doctors' injunctions, so it seemed, were the worst kind of worldly injustice to be inflicted upon one of the greatest champions of humanity, so this was becoming a tragedy of Shakespearian proportions. But the physical frailties that Pulitzer was cursed with were inescapable, and though, as we will see, he found ways, to some degree, to circumvent them, he could not escape them. He was still building the twenty story skyscraper for the World that dwarfed the competition but, unfortunately, for the rest of his earthly days, he would only set foot in his castle of triumph a handful of times.

Because of his nervous afflictions, Pulitzer had to seek places to live where there was complete silence, and he spent more money doing so. The apartment building he rigged up for himself in Manhattan, for instance, where he lived infrequently, had to have the elevator reengineered several times to ensure that it was silent. This building was separate from where Kate raised the children, for Pulitzer could no way in hell endure the unending sounds of a normally developing family. Another home in Lakewood, New Jersey had a massive three story edifice beside the main building that became known to his secretaries as the Tower of Silence, because of its imposing possession of that elusive quality. Pulitzer also purchased a yacht, the same luxurious entity owned by many of the robber barons of the period, including stock swindler Jay Gould, but he did not own it for ostentation, but for the quiet and seclusion it could afford. Unfortunately, visiting many of the world's most beautiful places, which he, unfortunately, could not see, he often ran into the challenge that these places were not, as he wished, silent, so his yacht had to sail onward in search of more peaceful locations. (Alas, his petitions to stop the noise-making activities at these places, such as the morning artillery salutes during the raising of the flag in Naples, came to naught.) Unjust as it may have seemed, Charles Dana got his wish, and Pulitzer had to move on, moreover to wander the world in search of happiness that proved more and more elusive. Dana would never again be the Dean of newspaper owners of Manhattan, for the travelling Pulitzer would ensure that his newspaper had knocked Dana off of that perch for good.

The best way he could find to satisfy his thirst for information and, despite the orders of the doctors, supervise his newspapers, was by using a team of secretaries to act as his eyes and ears. These men, they were all men, needed to possess an array of qualities to serve the great journalistic craftsman, and some were rather urbane. A good secretary had to have a soft voice, and be able to travel noiselessly, perhaps with rubber soled shoes, if necessary. But other characteristics were far more substantial. Pulitzer loved to be read to, and was a lover of Shakespeare, and a good secretary had to do justice to a somewhat thespian reading of the Great Bard. Other things he wanted read were more pedestrian, such as novels, but a good secretary had to know how to edit what was read to the picky Hungarian. For Pulitzer was always in search of the facts, the facts, the facts, and novels with a lot of introductory information that Pulitzer would consider unnecessary would drive him up the wall to hear, so a good secretary had to know how to summarize this information in a few piquant sentences (remember condense!) and then get onto the more factual information of the plot.

The first residence that Pulitzer bought to provide relief from his new condition was off the beaten track up near Bar Harbor, Maine, way up the rugged coast of that out-of-the-way state. It was a comfortable little estate with a large granite residence sitting behind the gravel driveway lined with sycamore trees, with a peaceful brook flowing in back of the grounds. The largest noise problems were the occasional squawking of a passing flock of Canada geese or the night time whistling of cicadas, but Pulitzer's bedroom was insulated against these intrusions and he, mostly, enjoyed the silence of the deep country setting. Yet his hunger for information was rampant, and he pursued the search for secretaries relentlessly. Cockerill rode the train up from New York with a candidate for that position, and Pulitzer grilled the man remorselessly. Sitting behind an impressive mahogany desk wearing the thick sunglasses that would shield him from light for the rest of his earthly days, Pulitzer bluntly made his inquiries to assess the man's talent.

"So you want to be my secretary," the invalid declared. "Tell me about your reading tastes. Surely you have read Shakespeare, Plato and Rousseau."

"Well..." the applicant replied hesitantly.

"You know, as a secretary," Pulitzer stated, interrupting him, "that you'll have to read to me, and I want you not only to have a nice soft reading voice, but have knowledge of the material."

"I see."

"So go on, tell me."

"Tell you?" queried the applicant, having lost track of the thread of the conversation.

"About the authors I just mentioned and your reading tastes!"

"I know Shakespeare, Mr. Pulitzer, but–"

"Out right now, go. Good bye. Don't come back here and waste my time again like this, John. I need a man who can be my eyes and ears so I can run my newspapers and I will get him, Goddamnit!"

Thus Pulitzer, entrapped in the unenviable position of a man having great difficulty quenching his insatiable thirst for information, was a difficult man to satisfy, and often took out his frustration on those about him. No one got to know this better than Kate, who felt like a mere bystander up in Maine as Pulitzer did not spend his days as the doctors had ordered, but was his old workaholic self, having the World and the competing papers read to him, before he dictated off lengthy instructions about every facet and detail of every edition so the employees back in New York had not escaped from his voluminous ministrations. Either Cockerill or Frank White was up there getting the latest instructions, with hardly a moment's rest. When it came time for dinner, Kate did not find it a peaceful time, for her husband was still angry, nervous irritable, and dissatisfied with the meal's delivery.

"Damn it Claude," he had exclaimed. "I've told you numerous times to fix the squeak on that wheel! It is irritating!"

Kate felt helpless, as Pulitzer's irrational yet dictatorial behavior had deteriorated to an almost unmanageable level.

After returning to New York, she again sought out Davidson for advice.

"I've begun to feel like a single mother," she confessed.

"How is he handling things?" Davidson inquired.

"Not too well, Tom, he's very jumpy and nervous."

Davidson sympathized with her.

"It is hard for him to be alone like that," he theorized.

"But if he were here it would be way too much for him. The slightest things send him into a frenzy. The doctors are right, he needs to be secluded."

"Kate," said Davidson, attempting to console her.

She broke down in tears.

"He's a broken man."

"Oh, Kate, please don't say that."

"He sits up there with his secretary who reads to him. He's going to buy a yacht so he can sail off to God knows where and who knows when he'll come back."

"But his secretary helps him to run the papers, in a way."

"Oh Tom."

"You've got to help him too, Kate."

"Help him? I don't have the faintest idea how to run a newspaper."

"I don't mean that. Please pardon me for being so personal."

"Don't you think I've tried that through the years? He won't listen to a word of it."

"Now's your chance, Kate."

"My chance?"

"Think about it," Davidson advised, "he's at a low point, and you can reach him. But do it now, when his guard is down."

Kate ruminated about Davidson's suggestion on the train on the way back up to Bar Harbor, and rethought about how she might indeed help her husband because this was a difficult time. And perhaps she had to strike when the iron was hot. Perhaps because his physical constitution had failed him so abysmally he would be more willing to ask for help, and let down his often imposing know-it-all-manner. But, she thought, he still was an extremely talented man in many ways, and continued to blaze trails in journalism but now, with the new, added problems, he needed people to help him achieve those goals. And she could be one of the people to help him.

So the next night she spent with him in Maine, when the two reclined in the Bar Harbor master bedroom, she attempted a light conversation with him. She was finding out that what Tom said was true. In his loneliness and isolation he was so desperate for company he was more open to her than he might have formerly been.

"How's it going with the newspaper?" she inquired.

"That goddamn Hearst is so outrageous," Pulitzer lamented.

"It's kind of funny, isn't it?"

"Funny?!"

"Fireworks, festivals, parades, he's kind of like a little kid."

"Eh, maybe," Pulitzer grumbled.

"Come on, darling, what happened to your sense of humor? Sometimes you take things too damned seriously."

Kate grinned and covered her mouth, embarrassed that she had come out with a profanity.

"My goodness gracious!" Pulitzer blurted.

"Oops!"

"I have never heard you utter profanity!"

"Well it's not like you haven't."

"Well..."

"It will never happen again," she declared.

"Ha!"

"You know that I love you, darling, and I want to do my best to help you."

"Get me a new pair of eyeballs."

"I'll try."

\* \* \* \* \* \* \* \*

# Chapter 8

## A Circulation War

Time moved on, despite Pulitzer's trauma, and the world of newspaper journalism continued to expand. Pulitzer did his best to keep up with events going on at the World, and was constantly building his team of secretaries to enable him to get back to being his good old workaholic self. The first man to survive the grueling Pulitzer interview was a demure, British, middle aged gentleman, named Claude Ponsonby, who served him with tact and responsibility for many years. Another was Dr. Hosmer, who was dually qualified, as it was important to have a doctor about considering Pulitzer's weak physical constitution, and Hosmer was highly educated and well versed in current events as all secretaries had to be. They and a constantly changing team of men roamed the earth with Pulitzer, forever seeking new places of seclusion for the brilliant fugitive. The main source of relief from his boredom was conversation, and few were they who could keep up with his demanding requirements in that fine art. But once he had exhausted a secretary of topics to discuss he required new men, with new things to talk about, (or to pick their brains, some secretaries felt). Hence, there was a necessity for a constantly changing team.

Another of their tasks was to seek out places for short term rental across Europe suitable for their chief, as in free of noisy birds, barking dogs, loud children, etcetera, and nothing could get a secretary sent to the doghouse quicker than finding accommodations that later proved to have any of these annoyances. Pulitzer often had his team take him out to the theater, but such trips were often cut short, as there was no secretary on stage to instruct the cast to cut out introductory parts that could be summarized in a few discrete sentences. So Pulitzer and his entourage most often came back from their theater box at or even before intermission, and the team was more curious than Pulitzer as to what happened in the show they had bolted from. He also had a talent for not staying for the end of operas or concerts, and was driven to great anxiety by the normal interruptions of people coughing, rustling their programs or removing candy from paper bags.

His primary concern, however, was his newspapers and the news, and he kept his secretarial team jumping with the intense supervise-everybody-style they helped him to recapture from his former life. When on the yacht, Pulitzer arranged for all the most recent Worlds and the competing papers to be waiting for him at every port they passed, and once fetched aboard, these were read to him, including precise descriptions of pictures, advertisements and illustrations. Thereafter, regarding the World, Pulitzer would send telegrams and letters to the personnel. Telegrams were for immediate and pressing problems, and woe betide the employee who failed to respond to the directions. Letters were written most often to the upper level of editors, such as Cockerill and White, about long term issues such as Presidential prospects or the flow of editorial page columns regarding Tammany Hall. The secretarial team began to feel themselves as Pulitzer intended them to be, the eyes and ears of Joseph Pulitzer, the man at the top.

As the man at the top he had to control the structure of his newspapers, and interview and appoint the men who ran them. Because he was giving his orders through letters and telegrams, his system became similar to that of James Gordon Bennett, who, we recall, ran the Herald through telegrams. Bennett's system encouraged employees to spy and rat on each other to the boss, a system that some chided as relying on "white mice," or employees who would curry favor with the temperamental Bennett by disclosing uncompromising facts, real or imagined, about their fellow employees. It was quite different with Pulitzer, however, as when he received such information he would forward it to the employee who had been maligned and then referee the dispute. Such a system or course, discouraged inter-office backstabbing. Pulitzer came up with bureaucratic structures that made employees compete with each other in different and sometimes overlapping domains. Such a system caused men to either fight against each other in their relations, or draw boundaries of jurisdiction and ignore each other. In this respect Pulitzer was not good at promoting an atmosphere where his employees cooperated with each other. In choosing men for these positions, Pulitzer would interview the candidates himself, and enduring the probing questions from his great mind could often be a nerve-wracking experience. Pulitzer's desire that his employees devote themselves completely to their work (including during their free time) was enlarged by his desperate condition. Formerly he infected his employees with such enthusiasm by his own hard work and dynamic instruction so they would follow suit and do the same. But because he now relied on them to do at a distance what he could not, his thirst for their obedience became far more ruthless, and the lonely hours he spent in seclusion gave him ample time to construct complex supervisory dictums he grilled the candidates about in interviews. He would question them on their knowledge from local to international politics, the arts, reading, music and a range of journalistic skills, from reporting a story to arranging a crusade. It was not only their actions as editors he had strictures about, but how they had to spend much of their free time reading the papers of the competition, and other hours reading the classics to make them the highly cultured individuals he thought it necessary for them to be to promote excellence at the World. The Sunday World, which was the flagship of his news empire, could not be overseen by a team of shoddy charlatans. So a trip to Pulitzer's yacht or one of his mansions for an interview was invariably a torturous ordeal, and often the candidates felt themselves pushed to the marrow by this desperate genius. As the years wore on, and Pulitzer continued to keep close track of the World with an endless procession of letters and telegrams to ports he would pick up from his yacht or have delivered to his secluded residences of silence where his secretaries read their contents and faithfully recorded his responses. The employees of the Globe and Post-Dispatch felt his presence daily, though he was never there. Like a sometimes benevolent dictator, the presence of the greatest mind of journalism of his day was forever in the consciousness of the employees who worked in his wake.

Yet Hearst still plagued him with his paper down the street, and Pulitzer, like everyone else, initially thought that Hearst's wild inflation of the Pulitzer style would not last. As Hearst's successes continued on unabated through the years, Pulitzer came to realize this was not the case. He saw he was making the same mistake his competitors had when he came on the scene, in underestimating new competition because it was different. Hearst's methodology was merely an exaggeration of his own, so that it would work, and it was foolish to think otherwise. Yet Pulitzer, like some of his other competitors, saw that Hearst was losing lots of money in what seemed like wild and carefree investments, and hopefully thought it would come to an end. Hence, speaking to Cockerill in Maine, he declared,

"His mother has to cut him off from the family fortune soon. How long will she forbear him?"

"There's no sign of it stopping, Mr. Pulitzer," Cockerill replied.

"But he's losing a million a year!"

Unfortunately for Pulitzer, it was a statistical fact that the mining empire of Hearst's late father had given the young man what seemed like an inexhaustible fortune.

"But he's got hundreds of millions more to lose."

"God damn spoiled brat!" growled the angry Hungarian.

Though the years the competition see-sawed back and forth between the two sensationalists. In the Bowery, Pulitzer gave out charcoal in the winter and ice in the summer, only to be outdone by Hearst, who opened up soup kitchens year round and put up swimming pools for the summer. Pulitzer did not seek to imitate the wild fireworks shows that Hearst would put on year round, nor the brass band led parades down Columbus Avenue with ecstatic crowds cheering for the Journal. He tried a Yellow Balloon race from St. Louis to New York that would publicize both of his papers, but the weather did not cooperate, forcing the two balloons elsewhere. Hearst immediately and contemptuously began a coast to coast yellow feather race, between special passengers on two separate train lines, a race that did not depend upon favorable weather. In this spectacle crowds at train stations would squeal and cheer as the bright yellow bunch of feathers passed through, in a coast-to-coast self-promotion style news story where he used the same tricks Pulitzer had employed when Nellie had gone round the world. In the nationwide game, Hearst had by this time bought papers in Chicago and other cities in the Midwest, and was constructing the nationwide newspaper conglomerate of which Pulitzer had formerly dreamed. Before his breakdown Pulitzer had considered purchasing the Chicago Tribune, but it was Hearst who got it, leaving Pulitzer far behind. So when Hearst sponsored his yellow feather train passenger race, his nationwide syndicate of papers would have readers pick winners and losers and times the trains would arrive, so once again, Hearst had beaten Pulitzer at his own game.

With some news events, however, Hearst was letting this exaggeration color his coverage of the news, and this came to a head in the coverage of the Spanish American War, when America fought to kick Spain out of its colonies in Cuba, Puerto Rico and the Philippines in 1898. To Pulitzer, however, whether or not Hearst would beat him out in circulation became a more important issue than the truth of the news, so he stepped down in the gutter to fight with him. The two editors had a circulation war that is probably the most famous circulation war in newspaper history, as these two journalistic pugilists fought it out in their daily editions, and Pulitzer felt it necessary to keep his coverage as exciting as that of his ruthless rival.

Sitting at his mahogany desk in Maine one morning, he bristled while listening in an agitated manner as Ponsonby read to him from Hearst's paper, the Journal. The huge banner headline of the article read: SPAIN CRUEL IN CUBA.

"The cruel imperialist government of Spain must be thrown out of Cuba, and if that means war, so be it."

"That's enough, Claude," Pulitzer said, interrupting him. "We're going to have to hire some more lively reporters."

Pulitzer promptly dictated telegrams to the World to that effect.

Down at the paper Cockerill himself had a candidate in mind, though he had reservations about hiring him as he felt the young fellow was too much of a sensationalist. He had discussed it with White in a late night strategy session in the barroom.

"The boss wants new reporters, but this fellow Creelman from the Brooklyn Eagle is what I would call a potboiler reporter."

"Potboiler?" questioned White.

"In his stories, drama takes precedence over fact."

"Wouldn't this put us in danger of violating some of the principles the World was founded on?" White inquired.

"Indeed," said Cockerill grimly.

Cockerill's fears, however, were trumped by the orders from the top, so Creelman was recruited to join the staff of the World. He jumped at the opportunity, as the assignment to go down to Cuba, with the increased pay and excellent sensationalist opportunity, appealed to him very much.

Interviewing in Cockerill's office, Creelman queried as to his new responsibilities.

"So you want me to spice up the coverage about Cuba?" he inquired.

"Drama, Mr. Creelman, that's what we want, drama."

"There's no shortage of that down there," he replied.

So Creelman ventured down to Miami, where the chief source of news about Cuba was a crude sawdust-on-the-floor saloon where Cuban natives told tales that were more geared toward rallying support for the Cuban Revolution than reporting the facts. They billed themselves as eyewitnesses to the merciless cruelty of the Spanish oppressors, with stories that were, they remorselessly guaranteed, one hundred percent true. Evidence from this dubious news station came back in Creelman's first reportorial telegram that Cockerill read lethargically to Frank White. Following wild tales of Spanish soldiers raping innocent Cuban maidens followed by a few exacting descriptions of mutilation inflicted upon the heroic Cuban men who had tried to save them, Creelman summarized:

"No man's life, no man's property is safe. American property is destroyed on all sides. The horrors of the barbarous struggle for the extermination of the native population are witnessed in all parts of the country. Blood in the roadsides, blood in the fields, blood on the doorsteps, blood, blood, blood!"

"I think that qualifies as lively," White commented.

"Yup," assented Cockerill.

"Mr. Creelman is lowering us into the Hearstian cesspool of half-truth."

"Half-truths?"

"How about bullshit?"

"He could have written that without leaving town," Cockerill asserted.

"On a trip to the men's room."

"Frank, I've got to say, I want to beat out Hearst in circulation but, looking at this so called reporting, I don't feel that we should lower ourselves to Hearst's dishonest level of rabble-rousing in order to beat him."

"We might end up winning the battle and losing the war," said White.

So there began to be dissension in the ranks, as Cockerill and White came to feel that Pulitzer had lost sight of the quality of the World's journalism in this blind struggle to sell more papers. They felt that Pulitzer's fear of being overtaken by Hearst was blinding him from keeping to some of the bedrock principles that had been fundamental elements to the foundation of his newspapers. Perhaps in this regard, Pulitzer's absence from the workplace and indirect communication with his subordinates was not helpful.

Over at the Journal, Creelman's first reporting in the World did not escape Hearst's attention. His new paper had become, by this time, a New York institution, and the Journal building was a fully ensconced Hearst madhouse. Unlike Pulitzer's office, which had been overflowing with paperwork, Hearst's office was packed with knickknacks, souvenirs and memorabilia. Hearst, that morning, was showing one of the most notable items in his collection to Ambrose Bierce.

"Wait till you see this, Ambrose," he declared.

Reaching into a large wooden box he pulled out a long dress sword, the handle of which was encrusted with rubies and diamonds. Along the blade was a tribute was carved to Cuba's military leader, General Maximo Gomez.

"I'm going to take this with me down to Cuba," Hearst announced, "and, at the proper moment, present it to General Gomez, as a symbol of our support for his heroic revolution."

"He can cut off a few Spanish heads with it," Bierce proclaimed.

"Something else, Ambrose, have you read this guy Creelman who is working for the World?"

"He's got some stones, doesn't he?"

"Absolutely," Hearst declared. "We've got to get our people down there to hire him away from Pulitzer."

"Double the salary as usual?"

"Or triple it if you have to."

"We're going to hire some more people away from the mad Hungarian," Bierce contended.

"I must say, Ambrose, that Pulitzer was the man who blazed the trail. But he's a limited man."

"True."

"You need to have a killer instinct in this business."

"He is just an obstacle to us now," Bierce asserted.

"And we are going to have to shove him out of the way," Hearst declared.

Back up in Maine, Pulitzer was not pleased. As time went on, struggling to fend him off as he might, the assault from Hearst was becoming bizarre and unpredictable, putting Pulitzer on the defensive, and he was not used to that.

"Hearst has hired Creelman?" he queried his secretary incredulously.

"That's right, Mr. Pulitzer," Ponsonby confirmed.

"Can we offer him more money to hire him back?"

"The staff thinks, Mr. Pulitzer, that you can try but it will be difficult to find him down there. Hearst will probably send him to Cuba."

"Hearst is getting to be a real pain in the ass," Pulitzer lamented.

"I am afraid that that is not all of the bad news, sir."

"What else, pray tell?"

"Hearst has hired away the entire staff of the Sunday World."

"The whole staff? You have to be kidding."

"I wish that I were, Mr. Pulitzer."

Pulitzer did not have enough time to parade a whole team of potential Sunday News staff members through his Maine residence for interviews before the next edition was due.

\* \* \* \* \* \* \* \*

Ponsonby's prediction about what Hearst would do with Creelman proved correct, as Creelman was sent right to Havana. In the Hearst organization it was passion rather than seniority that was the basis for promotion, and Creelman was sent to take over for a man named Stan Tasker, whose reporting was judged to be lethargic in comparison. Creelman wasted no time in finding a dramatic story to pursue, and had Tasker waiting outside of the Recojidas Prison on the outskirts of Havana for him to emerge, as Tasker was now his assistant. The new chief of Cuban operations was finishing up an interview with a young female prisoner named Evangelina Cosio in the visiting quarters, while Tasker sweated in the mid-day sun on a buckboard outside.

"I hope that you can help me," the seventeen year old pleaded.

"I will do my best, Miss Cosio," Creelman replied.

"Thank you so much, Mr. Creelman," she beseeched dramatically as he exited.

A middle aged female guard raised her eyebrows in contempt at the young woman's histrionics.

Creelman gave Tasker a summary as they departed.

"Well, Sam, it's like this. Her father was under house arrest for revolutionary activities, and she set up an ambush to attack the guards in a failed escape attempt."

"Thus, she's here," concluded Tasker.

"Correct, with an impending twenty year sentence."

"I don't know if we can get much out of this," Tasker theorized.

"Au contraire, Amigo! This is a rich situation," Creelman instructed. "Do you know what my motto in life is?"

"Not yet."

"Never let truth get in the way of a good story."

"You don't say," said Tasker.

"Let me tell you what really happened. The Spanish soldiers barged into Miss Cosio's cottage and assaulted her with sexual advances, and when the virtuous young maiden resisted, she was arrested, and sent here."

"That sounds far more newsworthy," ventured Tasker.

"We have to get you on track with the methods of the Journal, Sam. Once Hearst's Sob Sisters get a hold on this one it will become a cause célèbre and a national crusade."

"Sob Sisters?" Tasker queried.

"That's our nickname for the female columnists."

Creelman, energetic young reporter that he was, had been studying the Hearst methodology for some time. Having done so, he was familiar with his responsibilities as the point man on the story in the Hearst publicity machine. He wrote an imaginative article about the gross injustice that the virtuous young maiden, Miss Cosio, was being subjected to, and the Sob Sisters got into action without delay. Mixing fiction, fact and melodrama in an intoxicating concoction, Cosio was portrayed as innocent maiden in Cuba whose honor was being prostrated by the horrifying Spanish authorities. Beatrice Fairfax, a columnist that Hearst had spirited away from the World, wrote:

## Cuba's Joan of Arc

Evangelina Cosio, dear readers, is a touching symbol of the villainous cruelty of the Spanish government toward the Cuban people. She is a young maiden, beautiful, as you can see from our drawing, who is forced to scrub floors in a filthy prison in Havana under the threat of torture. And what is her crime, pray tell? She defended her own person against the lustful advances of a Spanish officer who tried to force himself upon her! She was staying near her beloved father, a man unjustly imprisoned on trumped up charges, charges she protested against as unfair. In response, the Spanish sent in soldiers to shut her up, and the soldiers made bold sexual advances when they came upon her. She, like the innocent maiden she is, resisted, and what did they do? They again made trumped up charges and sent her to the horrifying Recojidas Prison in Havana. Does she have enough to eat? Heavens no, she is starving. Does she have enough clothes? No again, she wears rags that barely cover her while lustful evil Spanish Prison Guards subject her to forced labor and leave her undefended from the brutal prisoners there at night, wanton Negresses. Oh the injustice of it all!!!!

The entire front page was devoted to Miss Cosio, and portrayed her as a symbol of the rapacious greed and avarice with which Spain mercilessly treated the innocent and vulnerable Cuban population. Once the public sympathies were aroused in this soap opera dynamic, the Hearst machine moved onward by having their thousands of stringers circulate petitions to protest the injustice of the young maiden's problem. They were instructed to seek out women, and concentrate on the most famous ones in their venues across the country, noting the names of the most prominent signers when they sent in the petitions. The stringers were successful and signed up, with hundreds of thousands of others, some nationally prominent women, such as the widows of Ulysses Grant and the former President of the Confederacy, Jefferson Davis. Julia Ward Howe, author of the Battle Hymn of the Republic, signed the petition, as did Clara Barton, the heroic nurse from the Civil War and founder of the Red Cross. Hearst had aroused public sympathy to an extraordinary degree.

"Goddamn charade extraordinaire," Pulitzer exclaimed to Ponsonby up in Maine, "Hearst is orchestrating a veritable newspaper circus."

Pulitzer suddenly found himself in league with the men he had formerly regarded as sedentary and boring newspaper chieftains. They had all investigated the affair and found it a hoax, and loudly documented the outrageous fabrication in their own papers. But Hearst had taken the country by storm, and their protests were largely ignored by the national avalanche of public sentiment. It was the same with the protests of the Spanish government, who vigorously objected through the diplomatic process, but found that truth and reason were taking a back seat to emotion and melodrama. Since these efforts failed, Spain planned to pardon and free the young maiden, and get this major league headache off of the front page.

William Randolph Hearst, however, well informed of the realities of the situation, saw the potential roadblock of the Spanish pardon coming, and quickly moved to circumvent it. Would not the public be ecstatic if the Hearst reporters themselves freed Miss Cosio? Absolutely! Creative minds in New York wrote up a tale of the escape which involved hack saws sawing through the hated prison bars, (by the exhausted and overworked Miss Cosio, late into the night, sawing away for her freedom), ladders leading across the prison roof to, what else, a trellis for the young lady to climb down to be carted off to her well-deserved freedom. At the same time that imaginative Hearst writers were sketching out this dangerous escape, a more reliable method was being employed: bribery. Emissaries were sent to the local watering hole were the prison guards were regulars and arranged for implementing this time honored tradition. Creelman himself performed the payoff, as Tasker waited outside again, this time as a passenger in a four-in-hand, as Creelman went into the prison carrying the prearranged bag of gold coins. Inside the prison he talked to the female prison guard who previously was contemptuous of Miss Cosio's maudlin acting performances.

"Here it is, as we agreed," murmured Creelman, handing over the prearranged bag of gold coins.

"Thank you, Amigo," she replied, and Miss Cosio emerged silently to accompany Creelman out the back door through the darkness, in a not so daring escape.

The Journal had full diagrams of the valiant escape from the maiden's cell window, across the roof and down the trellis on the front page, and Joseph Pulitzer sat seething listening to this demented depiction being read to him by Claude Ponsonby.

"After a dangerous climb over the ladders across the roof, her tender hands calloused from her slaving away with a hacksaw on the iron prison bars of her cell, Miss Cosio approached a trellis that was, as pictured in the drawing, right next to the entrance to the prison! She could have been captured at any moment! Fortunately freedom was her fate and she was able to climb down the trellis to be spirited away by the heroic revolutionaries of the Journal."

"PT Barnum has nothing on this guy," Pulitzer commented.

"It is a big charade," Ponsonby agreed.

"He stole his techniques from me, the little twerp," Pulitzer lamented.

"Perhaps, in an odd way, Mr. Pulitzer, his success in this charade is a compliment to your methodology."

Pulitzer did not acknowledge this long-winded compliment.

"I suppose he'll have fireworks again," he theorized.

Pulitzer's theory was correct. When Creelman and Miss Cosio came down the gangplank from their boat in New York Harbor, out of control crowds gave them an exceptionally warm reception. A path was cleared for their carriage to pull into a parade that awaited them, led by a brass band that took them down the streets of Manhattan past equally noisy crowds to a city park near Broadway where, as Creelman assisted the young maiden in climbing the stairs to the podium, red, white and blue fireworks blasted skyward to celebrate this glorious triumph for freedom and democracy. Creelman, it is probably safe to say, was enjoying his new employment very much. But the effect of Hearst's fairy tale did not end there. President William McKinley, even though he detested the story and knew it to be at variance with the facts, could not ignore the national sentiment. Advised by his handlers there were political gains to be had that he would be a fool to ignore, he took advantage of the opportunity. Miss Cosio was invited to attend a reception in her honor at the White House, where Hearst's reporters would broadcast this ceremony to the nation.

\* \* \* \* \* \* \* \*

After Hearst had drained all he could out of that dubious story another event fell right into his lap. The American battleship the Maine was sitting peacefully in the harbor of Havana, representing President McKinley's restrained attitude toward the conflict at hand. The peace of that February evening was irrevocably altered when, with no preliminary warning, the front of the boat exploded in a huge fireball killing 266 American sailors. As there was no combat of any kind beforehand, the explosion was a complete surprise, and the Spanish Navy were very helpful in helping to rescue the Americans who survived the explosion. The Captain of the boat was in the Spanish headquarters when he sent a telegram urging America to suspend judgment until the accident could be investigated. Unfortunately, reason and truth would again have to take a back seat to the new explosive journalism that Hearst was disseminating regarding the Spanish American War.

At the Journal, news of the explosion was like pixie dust on the fairies of the newspaper world, inspiring them to magical tasks at hand. Hearst sat gleefully at his desk reading the cables from Cuba, and called out to Bierce celebrate this rich little nugget of news.

"We've got Spain now!" he cried out.

"Absolutely," affirmed Bierce.

"Waddya think, Ambrose?"

"I've thought up a slogan, Chief!"

"Do tell!"

"Remember the Maine!"

Hearst burst up, suddenly filled with inspiration, and bounded into the hallway to pass on his enthusiasm to his staff.

"That's great, Ambrose," he proclaimed. "Remember the Maine, everybody! Remember the Maine! Get O'Neill in here, we've got to draw up pictures of how the Spaniards rigged the mine that blew up the Maine."

So began the Hearst news combine's ratcheting up of the pro-war hysteria with unbridled enthusiasm. For a news organization expanding the limits of sensationalism regularly, the Maine explosion added high octane fuel to the fire, and Hearst was not a man to miss a chance handed to him on a silver platter.

Back up in Maine, Pulitzer saw the ramifications and threat to his own news power as Ponsonby described the banner headline: REMEMBER THE MAINE- WAR WITH SPAIN, and read to him from the article. Underneath the banner headline was a large drawing that purported to show the mines with wires that the Spanish had placed on the bottom of the Maine.

"If Americans don't rise up and kick the Spaniards out of Cuba there will be no end to European interference in our hemisphere. We must fight, now!"

"That's enough, Claude," said Pulitzer, interrupting him. "Let's get packed up, I am going to New York."

This declaration from Pulitzer was a major departure from all dictates of his doctors. Pulitzer had disobeyed the strictures of staying in a dark room frequently, but this move was a more major departure. It was impossible for him, determined journalist he was, not to be on the scene at this critical juncture.

\* \* \* \* \* \* \* \*

In New York, entering his mighty skyscraper for the first time, he was led around on a tour, but could not help but to feel like a strange newcomer in the thriving newspaper emporium. There was an uncomfortable silence amongst the staff as he was led about the building by Cockerill and White, which he promptly reprimanded them for.

"This isn't a church, Goddamnit! Isn't there anyone working around here? When I was in charge at the World the place was filled with action and adventure! Do not think that you have to bow down like lackeys because I am here! Get to work!!!"

A nervous chatter started as the tour went on.

When he sat down in Cockerill's office to discuss editorial matters, however, he was quickly acquainted with the dissension in the ranks when Cockerill argued with him about the wisdom of a war with Hearst.

"Mr. Pulitzer, do you think a circulation war with Hearst is the right thing to do?" Cockerill inquired.

"We can't let him beat us in circulation, John! You of all people should know that after all these years."

"Mr. Pulitzer, as you once told me, accuracy is to a newspaper what chastity is to a woman, and once lost, can never be regained."

"This is about leadership, John, and we can't back down. The country is so riled up about war— if we lose on this issue, he, Hearst, will have the leading newspaper in New York."

"But he's leading us into the rat hole of untruth," Cockerill protested, "if we stay on our present course."

"Rat hole? John, you know that that's not true and some arguments for the invasion of Cuba are sound. The Concentration Camps, for instance."

Pulitzer was referring to the reports of Cuban Revolutionaries living in Spanish Concentration Camps, where thousands died.

"You know better that anyone that if we have a circulation war with him that intelligent debate will go out the window and we'll resort to the same kind of fraud that he is using-"

"John, you know that he is stealing our reporters."

"We've stolen reporters."

"But he's stealing whole staffs at a time."

"You should know what an unprincipled little shit he is who will stop at nothing to get ahead."

"All the more reason he should be stopped," Pulitzer declared.

"We won't be stopping him, we'll be promoting him!" Cockerill countered. "We'll be validating his sensationalist crusade, when we should be criticizing it."

"We can do that, in part."

"I am not so sure, Mr. Pulitzer."

"But John, look we're already in— there's no turning back— look at the stuff we printed with Creelman."

"His man now."

Pulitzer had grown increasingly frustrated during the conversation. He had come down to New York to get everyone on the same page, and his top man was disagreeing with him. How was he going to stay on top of the heap if his team were not united?

"That's it, Mr. Cockerill, I have had enough. You are fired."

"What?" questioned Cockerill incredulously.

"I need a reliable team, and if you are not going to support my efforts you can work somewhere else."

"You are kidding?!?"

"Get out."

Cockerill was dumbfounded. He had been trying to get Mr. Pulitzer back on course, and did not think that the invalid was in full possession of his faculties. It would be possible to do what he said, to criticize Hearst and keep a distance, but he did not think that Pulitzer was quite on the right path to do so. It could not be done by hiring people like Creelman, and his departure was good, not bad. But the moves that Pulitzer had been advising lately, like joining Hearst in the Remember the Maine campaign, Cockerill took issue with. He firmly believed that Pulitzer had lost his grip. And what was he to do? Go work for Hearst? He walked forlornly down the hallway to the elevator of the skyscraper, feeling the uneasy silence of his now former coworkers, went down, and out onto the street.

\* \* \* \* \* \* \* \*

At the Journal, Hearst was packing up to make his own personal trip down to Cuba, squirreling away memorabilia to take on the trip with him, when Ambrose Bierce barged into his office.

"Pulitzer's in town," Bierce proclaimed.

"Get out!" Hearst replied.

"He got in yesterday."

"Well, well, Ambrose, as I am going south, you are going to have to be my ambassador."

"To go see the old goat?" Bierce questioned maliciously.

"It is the kind of job that you delight in, is it not?"

Bierce chuckled with a sly grin on his face.

"You know me too well."

"Speaking of goats, Ambrose, your job will be to get his."

"It will be like shooting fish in a barrel."

The sardonic Bierce was a very effective instrument for Hearst in this kind of endeavor, as Hearst was, in person, the nicest guy you'd ever want to meet. But at a distance it could be quite a different matter, and Bierce was a very effective agent for him in that regard. Hearst and Bierce had a Yin-Yang going because their temperaments were symbiotic in their relationship. Bierce needed the stability of Hearst because he provided a very generous paycheck, although sometimes he had gotten drunk and quit in a huff, deriding his supposedly former boss, yet Hearst would hire him back, with a raise, to boot. But Hearst, the gentleman, needed Bierce, the antagonist, the provocateur, the obnoxious attacker; in these and many other ways Bierce was an instrument for Hearst, and he used him as a tool of attack. The rich miner's son did not have the gall to confront people without reserve like Bierce did. In this circulation battle, with Pulitzer in town, Bierce would be the perfect weapon to attack the old fool at his weakest, and Hearst was not the type of man to miss an opportunity like this.

Pulitzer viewed the conflict in a far different way, regarding himself as a man who made his own fortune and was not a crude impostor using his family's riches. He had hopes that Hearst would soon be shut off from the fortune, since Hearst's father, the man who had acquired it, was dead. His mother, Phoebe, Pulitzer continued to hope, would soon tie up the purse strings, so to speak, for he had spent himself, it was estimated, eight million dollars in debt promoting the Journal in New York. Surely such a prodigal son would be called to account at some point, and Hearst's lavish expenses could not go on this way ad infinitum.

What was unique about this circulation war was that it was not profitable for either Hearst or Pulitzer, as the lavish expenses being incurred got rid of the profits. Both men, for instance, hired celebrity columnists and reporters that were expensive, as well as printing the endless extra editions printed up to proclaim "new" news ("Extra, Extra, read all about it!!) which often had a majority of the copies returned to shop unsold. To get news out of Cuba, boats had to be hired to transport the news in and out to avoid the Spanish censors. Cable and transport fees were exorbitant, and Hearst's histrionics, firework shows, etc., were not cheap. As disdainful as Pulitzer was of such wild expenses, he joined Hearst in this pandemonium of newspaper extremism, and the contest drained his pocket as much as that of his rival.

Pulitzer's former bosses, Davidson and Schurz, were not pleased with the direction that Pulitzer's newspaper had taken. They had long ago acceded to his sensationalistic tactics, but the direction of his reporting on the Spanish American War was something they could not condone, especially Carl Schurz. The two discussed their former protégé's efforts in Schurz's uptown office.

"It's a circulation war," Davidson explained.

"That is going to create an all too real and unnecessary war," Schurz proclaimed.

"He thinks that Hearst is irresponsible."

"So that makes it okay for him?"

Schurz had grave misgivings about what he regarded as a line being crossed, when newspapers disregarded the facts and whipped up patriotic enthusiasm to sell papers with no feeling of responsibility for the consequences of their actions. He had sympathized with Pulitzer after his breakdown, and would grant him some largesse due to what he regarded as difficult physical and emotional limitations. Schurz could not go so far, however, as to grant Pulitzer license to engage in irresponsible journalism because of his condition, and intended to call a spade a spade unless there were some unlikely change in the direction of new affairs.

Back in the domestic arena, Pulitzer encountered yet another opponent to his circulation war, as Kate was not pleased with this direct disobedience of his doctors' orders. As Ponsonby guided him down the stairs to take him to the World for his first full day of work, Kate voiced her opposition.

"You know that your doctors have told you not to go to work like this, darling."

"Damn the doctors," he grunted in return.

"Don't they know about your health?"

"This is about the United States going to war with another nation."

"Are you sure that it's not about newspaper sales?"

"Certainly not!" he growled, as Ponsonby could not quite get to the door on time as the aging news titan barreled forward and barged recklessly through it.

How tragicomic it seemed to Kate. As she had gotten to know her husband through the years, she recognized his strengths and his weaknesses. His strengths were his Napoleonic ambitions and unique abilities to see and take advantage of opportunities that other men were blind to. His success in New York was ample evidence of this, where he took on crushing debt to buy a paper in what the news fraternity considered irrational to the point of insanity, yet he transformed the paper into the most popular one in the country, leaving the news fraternity in his wake. The battle with Hearst showed his weakness, and now, sadly, tragically, he stormed onward in an engagement he could not win, against a man who was younger and better supplied with an outside income that Pulitzer could not match— a man who imitated and enlarged the Pulitzer style to absurd proportions and that the public accepted without reservation. Joseph Pulitzer was being buried by an avalanche he himself had created, yet he could not see it, and fought with his own relentless and inescapable self-will for the control of a world that was indifferent to his grandiose ambitions. In such a case his egotistical power lust seemed foolish to the extreme, and he was blind to the absurdity of his own insanity, like a man with his fly down who is the last one to find out. Kate resigned herself in sadness at her own inability to influence her mate, and saw he must learn these difficult lessons in the boxing ring of life that was his only true teacher. As brilliant a man as he was he was emotionally very limited, and failed to recognize that his own spot in the limelight of human existence was mortal in scope, and that trying to enlarge it beyond its earthly proportions was a fatal task . She had tried, with limited success, to take advantage of the chance to help her husband in his moment of weakness as Thomas Davidson had suggested, but as time went on such efforts could only go so far. Joseph Pulitzer was a man with a unique path of fate he had launched himself on and was, to a large degree, a prisoner to his own self-will. Kate came to feel she could do no more to help him than a nurse at the hospital of a wounded war veteran, yet this veteran barged back onto the battlefield despite his bandages and his crutches, determined to win the war single handedly by charging though the battlefield of mortars and machine guns lined up against him that made his crude self-determination look ridiculous. Yet he would do what he would do, and she was far from the only person to recognize it.

\* \* \* \* \* \* \* \*

Back in France, Bennett lounged on his bed surveying the circulation war of the two news titans, and had a similar take on the pomposity of his two rivals.

"Take this off and send it off to the Herald right away, Clarence," he announced, as Clarence pulled out his shorthand pad.

"To all employees of the Herald:

"It is now our duty to counteract the offensive, untruthful and heretical news coming out of both Hearst and Pulitzer's papers. When these two childish and explosive journalists throw confetti like news in the air it is one thing, but when they give out false news and bad advice that turns into misdirected foreign policy it is quite another. All responsible individuals in both the American and Spanish governments counsel patience and inquiry into events and that is the course we must preach. This is a very important time for us to put out the fire before it catches on and burns us all."

"I'll cable this off immediately," said Clarence.

"Rouse out the crew, Clarence, and have the yacht brought around. We'll be leaving today."

\* \* \* \* \* \* \* \*

In the Dome, the top stories of the World headquarters where the reporters' desks were located, Pulitzer was seated in the middle in a sort of improvised throne, where White and other staffers attempted to coordinate his interactions with the staff. There was an air of unease in the office, as this new and improvised situation seemed queer and unusual to the office regulars. There was also a communal shock that Cockerill had been fired, and unease and nervousness that the temperamental Pulitzer would fire other people in the Dome. Pulitzer attempted to recreate the energy and creativity he had formerly infected his staff with. Trouble was that it had been many a day since he had been the man springing around the shop spreading enthusiasm with his own boundless energy, and few were the veterans, especially with the defections to Hearst, who could remember Pulitzer in his prime. Pulitzer was no longer the man he once was, and to new employees who had known him only from letters and telegrams he was only a sultan from afar. In person, unfortunately, they saw only his bad points, his dissatisfactions, and his predilection to perceive the rest of the world as on a lower and inferior plane than himself. He was overbearing, irritable, vengeful and vindictive toward staff members, who had difficulty maintaining the charity they were willing to grant him as an invalid. The vast majority of the staff did not have the patience to deal with this singular creature like his secretarial team did, and unfortunately came to regard him as an intrusive and unnecessary pain in the ass. The general feeling on the staff was that he was better at running the paper, in his current condition, from afar through letters and telegrams. In that way he could think out his responses and question people more intelligently. When he sat in the office the things that irritated him and small details took his attention away from his talent and intelligence, and his anger at the circulation war with Hearst led him to decisions not on par with his formerly high standards.

"Your story is inordinately long and goddamned boring!" Pulitzer fumed at a cub reporter who he had ordered to be summonsed before him. "Don't you know how to condense a compelling story beneath a fascinating headline?!"

The timid young man shook in his boots, afraid to respond.

"Well!?"

"I'm sorry, Mr. Pulitzer, it's only a first draft—"

"It better be, you bozo, now look, here's the headline: Canned rations poison soldiers. Now come back when you've got something worth reading."

The cub slunk off, and Pulitzer listened to White read him the next proposed article that would be the object of his wrath.

While Pulitzer was charting the course of the circulation war, one of his chief enemies, a much younger man, Theodore Roosevelt, was gallivanting into the war creation business like a carefree college student quaffing beers at a fraternity initiation. After the explosion of the Maine Roosevelt promptly resigned as Assistant Secretary of the Navy and enrolled in the US Army to form what became probably the most publically recruited company in the history of the US Army. He named them the Rough Riders, a romping cavalry battalion which was a combination of ex-football players, Yale and Harvard athletes, tobacco chewing cowboys and an assortment of other varieties of tough guys who wanted to become stars in the American pantheon of war heroes. Many were called but few were chosen to be part of this heroic fraternity, who promptly made camp near Amarillo, Texas, where Roosevelt trained them to coordinate their various horse riding styles into being able to stampede as a colossal brigade that shook the skies. Supervised by General Wood, the man later under him as chief of staff at the White House, Roosevelt ran a tough camp of patriotic discipline. After hours, however, a significant contingent of more bawdy individuals snuck off to the saloons of Amarillo for different gallivanting, to return soon enough for their rigorous training at the crack of dawn. This patriotic display was a theatrical extravaganza that Theodore Roosevelt would use to propel him toward the Presidency, and he excelled in his military service like a child devotedly enthralled in a very important game. For Theodore Roosevelt never lost the innocent joy and idealism of his childhood, and embraced America's patriotic frenzy to get rid of those darn Spaniards as a hero of the highest caliber. With this preparation, in Pulitzer's opinion, Roosevelt was ready to use the Spanish American War as a theatrical vehicle to propel his political career onto the national stage.

The patriotic wave that Roosevelt was riding, you might say, was very strong. As public sentiment and patriotic fever intensified, the reticence of President McKinley for war was overpowered by the strength of the national sentiment. Theodore Roosevelt, lowly former Undersecretary of the Navy, had a strident desire to turn the United States into an international powerhouse. With the help of Hearst and Pulitzer, the nation became geared up for war, so the vote in Congress reflected the patriotic fervor.

Davidson and White reminisced about the recent votes in Congress about the upcoming war at the World.

"The vote in the Senate was close, I understand," Davidson observed.

"A seven vote difference," White responded.

"But the House was a wash?"

"Three hundred and nine to seven."

"I guess you could say that the country is riled up."

"Yup," said White.

"You might say that you all have started up more than a circulation war."

\* \* \* \* \* \* \* \*

William Randolph Hearst, it should be said, was another man who never outgrew the disposition from his childhood days when he fooled his parents with the bathroom flare-fire. He came to view the world, to some degree, as his own personal playground, and the Spanish American War was no exception. He was somewhat the childish adventurer, when, off of the coast of Florida, he ordered his cruise boat to pull alongside of one of the Navy troopships that transported Theodore Roosevelt's Rough Riders and their horses. Well, only some of their horses, unfortunately, were along for the ride. Logistical problems had caused the Army to relate the tragic news that the flotilla only had enough room for half of the horses of these valiant heroes. So many of the Rough Riders found out that they would have to be rough walkers, and were sad and angry. As they sailed onward, the hold filled with grumbling men playing cards or other diversions, impatient for their upcoming military adventure, two Naval officers were standing at the starboard rail watching the approach of a much smaller cruiser, a boat with a man frantically trying to get their attention. The man was shouting at them through a large cone.

"Hello soldiers!" he cried out, "I am William Randolph Hearst of the newspaper the Journal in New York. I salute you in this war of liberation, and have here a valuable and inscribed dress sword that we would like you to present to General Gomez of the revolutionary forces as a sign of America's devotion to his cause. Could you take it, please?"

Hearst had not considered that a troop transport ship would not prioritize his offer enough to stop the ships and send a transport over and back to retrieve the sword, which would cause a significant delay in their timetable, plus all of the diplomatic telegrams and paperwork to get the permission to present the sword, amongst other difficulties.

"What's he saying?" queried one officer to the other.

"He's offering us a ceremonial sword to present to General Gomez."

"And that's the guy who owns the Journal in New York?!"

"Yup."

"God help us."

Undeterred by this refusal, Hearst continued to shadow the Naval Fleet on their trip to Cuba, and, upon arrival, placed his craft within hailing distance of their moorings. Thus Creelman and a photographer were onshore when the Rough Riders landed and were getting ready for their trip into the Cuban mainland. Roosevelt was certainly not shy for some wartime publicity, and gratefully took the opportunity, jovially responding to Creelman's questions about his optimism that they would kick those dastardly invaders back to Spain where they belonged. Teddy got down on one knee beside one of his platoons for a photograph, broadcasting the magnetic smile of his world famous and dynamic teeth.

"We will ride rough to victory men, shall we not?"

The Rough Riders responded with yessirs, catcalls, cheers, and grunts that they would.

Back at the Dome, two days later, when the story appeared, Pulitzer was not impressed.

"It probably looks like a Boy Scout picture," he barked.

"That it does, Mr. Pulitzer," White responded.

"He's a glory-goddamn-seeking bastard."

"Shall we call him the silk-stockinged soldier, Mr. Pulitzer?"

\* \* \* \* \* \* \* \*

Carl Schurz was making his opinions known that evening in a speech at the Union Club, determined to rally the civilized world against what he regarded as a barbaric and unnecessary war. This cultural den of the intelligentsia was packed to the gills for his speech, as Schurz wasn't the only one who felt that the yellow journals, as Hearst and Pulitzer's papers had begun to be called, were not being responsible in their news coverage. Schurz felt, however, deep down, that his troops, so to speak, were miniscule in number compared to the hordes that rallied pro-war nationally with the pot-boiling sheets of Pulitzer and Hearst.

"Nothing so disgraceful," Schurz declared, "as the behavior of these two newspapers in the past week has ever been known in the history of American journalism. Their gross misrepresentation of the facts and deliberate recklessness in construction of headlines has brought about outright rabble-rousing that makes this a very sad day for the United States of America. No one— absolutely no one— supposes that a yellow journal cares five cents about the Cubans, the Maine victims, or anyone else. The yellow journal is probably the nearest approach to hell existing in any Christian state."

Despite the passion of Schurz's speech, America was gripped by war fever, and could not wait to hear about it as the Rough Riders marched inland toward the concentrations of Spanish troops at Santiago. Climbing up and down the tropical mountain forests they forged inland, learning the difficulties of strenuous exercise in the humid and tropical climate. Eventually they came to a ridge where they were spotted by the enemy, who fired on them from across the valley with their Mauser Rifles, inflicting casualties. The Spanish strategy was to hold them up in the mountains until tropical diseases such as malaria took a toll on their ranks, and the Americans would give up. There were other obstacles to American troops which were self-inflicted, such as the non-tropical woolen uniforms better for Arctic fighting, and the tins of meat, some of which were poisonous to some unfortunate diners. American forces did not let these obstacles deter them from the campaign they were engaged in, though, and their American determination to fight led them out of the jungles toward direct confrontations with the Spanish Army that awaited them.

Both Hearst and Pulitzer had hired celebrity reporters to satisfy the public thirst for descriptions of the action of the war. Hearst's man was Richard Harding Davis, who was already a national celebrity and ladies' man for his short stories about romance and adventure. His narrations of the perils of adolescent young men who risked their very lives to save some hero who was being subjected to unjust dangers were very popular with female readers, who also felt an attraction to the handsome author himself as he was pictured in the magazines where they read his stories. Davis was a man very conscious of his own image, and once caused his journalistic colleagues to laugh him off the stage, so to speak, when he inquired, while reporting the devastating flood of Johnstown, Pennsylvania, where he could get a pressed and cleaned shirt. As almost the entire town had been washed away by the broken dam, this seemed a preposterous question, and his fellow reporters laughed at what they regarded to be a callow and insensitive question from a self-centered young reporter. In Cuba, though, almost ten years later, Davis had become a much more seasoned correspondent, and Hearst had financed appropriate clothing to enhance his appearance. Following the Rough Riders he was far more ready for the camera in his made-for-the-tropics khaki outfit topped by a wide brimmed hat than the soldiers, who sweated profusely in their dark woolen fatigues, which were more appropriate for battle in the frigid winters of Siberia. In this premier performance as a war reporter, he pumped up the drama of Theodore Roosevelt's war adventures to the utmost, and helped create the image that enabled Roosevelt to use the war as a political springboard to the Presidency. Roosevelt himself, well aware of the political possibilities he might reap from his participation in this great global struggle, was glad to have a reporter willing to idolize him free of the snide criticism he received from Pulitzer. Colonel Roosevelt made sure that Davis had a box seat to witness his famous ride up San Juan Hill, and Davis returned the favor in spades.

"Roosevelt," Davis wrote, "mounted high on horseback, and charging the rifle pits at a gallop and quite alone, made one feel that you would like to cheer. He wore on his sombrero a blue polka-dot handkerchief, which, as he advanced, floated out straight behind his head. Afterward, the men of his regiment who followed adopted a polka-dot handkerchief as a badge of the Rough Riders."

This glorification of Theodore Roosevelt did not sit well with Pulitzer.

"Sounds like that prick is rooting at a Goddamn football game!" the old man snarled from his throne in the Dome.

Pulitzer countered by hiring Stephen Crane as his celebrity newsman, the author who was famous for his realistic novel of the horrors of the Civil War, The Red Badge of Courage. Crane was realistic in his coverage of the war, though his objectivity was not seen in the fog of war, so to speak. He took a broader view of the charge up San Juan Hill than Davis' eyewitness account, and asserted that the famous charge was necessary to cover for the inglorious retreat of New York's 71st Division. While Davis' account may have been factually correct, Pulitzer found out that he would lose the dispute on more emotional grounds, and Hearst was quick to go for the jugular.

Hearst immediately attacked Pulitzer's patriotism, and headlines of the Journal blasted Pulitzer by name. "PULITZER QUESTIONS PATRIOTISM OF NEW YORK 71ST???" Hearst devoted three issues to attack his rival, including quotes from Roosevelt that the 71st were patriotic while pointing out that many of their number had fallen in battle. Pulitzer quickly realized the trap he had fallen into, and had to make mealy mouthed praises of the 71st, which Hearst derided him for. Once again, Pulitzer was being beaten at his own game.

Down in Cuba, Creelman was with Hearst on his cruise boat, and the two were present in the Harbor of Havana to watch as the American Navy shelled the ships of the Spanish Navy, in a turkey shoot against vastly inferior forces. Hearst and Creelman watched with glee as the mighty metal ships of the American Navy shelled the wooden sailboats of the Spanish Navy without mercy. Some Spanish sailors who survived the bombardment swam toward Hearst's boat.

"I think that they want to come aboard," Hearst remarked.

"They're probably safer here than they'd be in the hands of Cuban partisans on shore," opined Creelman.

"We're part of the war now, aren't we, James?"

Creelman reached over the rail to grasp the hand of one of the sailors and pull him on board.

"Indeed we are, Mr. Hearst."

"We'll have to send a telegram to your former boss."

Back at the Dome the next day, Pulitzer sat sternly listening as White read him the telegram.

"Welcome to my war, Mr. Pulitzer. Wish you were here. William Randolph Hearst."

"To hell with Hearst!" Pulitzer exclaimed, his face turning red as a beet.

On another war promotion front Pulitzer was not doing well, as Nellie Bly's efforts to recruit women volunteers was not receiving much interest. She stood forlornly at her booth on Columbus Avenue, bereft of volunteers, as Thomas Davidson approached to talk to her.

"I guess women aren't that eager to fight," she lamented.

"Not a single volunteer?" Davidson asked.

"A few ask, but they don't volunteer, or say they will, and don't come back."

"Ah well."

"On the other hand I've gotten harassed by a few Victorian women."

"They don't believe in women as soldiers or reporters, I suppose."

"Indeed not."

\* \* \* \* \* \* \*

Manhattan at that time had two distinct and interesting neighborhoods known as the Tenderloin and Hell's Kitchen, and they existed side by side in the middle portion of the island. The Tenderloin was where the well to do went for fun, including theater, fine restaurants, exclusive saloons and other emporiums of high class entertainment where satin gowns and silk top hats carried the day. Beside it was Hell's Kitchen, where the lower orders of society resided, and the crowded tenements that Pulitzer excoriated were clumped together on crowded avenues. This neighborhood, too, had scores of places for entertainment, including low class saloons, bordellos, illegal gambling dens and after hours "clubs." On the border of these two unique areas there were places that were sort of in between, as in not stuffy enough for the upper crust, but not lowly enough to attract muggers and thugs. One such den of iniquity was called Van Winkle's Nest, and it served a lot of beer and hard liquor in the late night hours.

There, in the dead of night, that time after the normal partying crowd had long departed for their beds, remained the real late nighters who, with a lifestyle somewhat similar to Dracula, most often did not end their revelries until the town began to lighten up with the approach of dawn. Two of these men were James Gordon Bennett and Ambrose Bierce, who happened upon each other in the Nest, as people called it, sitting a stool apart and having a spirited and adversarial conversation. It was getting near closing time on a Tuesday night, and the two late-night comrades sat alone near the end of the bar, sophisticates that they were, with brandy snifters and cigars. Bierce had bragged about his upcoming visit to Joseph Pulitzer.

"What the hell are you going to say to him?" Bennett inquired.

"What's the difference?" snorted Bierce. "The old goat is so jumpy that it doesn't take much to rile him up."

"You're right, what the hell is the difference, you guys are just as bad as he is."

"What the hell do you mean by that?!" Bierce countered.

"Well, to start with, despite your inflammatory so-called news styles, the circulation of your two papers is about the same as before, and mine is rising."

Bennett's little nugget of information was true, for the Herald's rational analysis of the war had gained his paper readers, while Pulitzer and Hearst's numbers, despite their flamboyance, stayed about the same.

"That's a flat out lie!"

"Have you checked the figures?" Bennett inquired insolently.

"I don't have to."

"Well forgive me. You want to stay ignorant just like your readers, who you have led into a stupid war that will haunt the US for years to come."

"You must not have heard of the Monroe Doctrine, you bozo."

"Oh sure," drawled Bennett, waving his cigar in the air, "forget negotiations, just bring out the army."

"Face it, Bennett, you're just jealous."

"Jealous of a rabble rousing half-wit? Hardly."

This assertion was too much for Ambrose Bierce, who vaulted off of his barstool and lunged at Bennett, toppling him and his barstool onto the unsanitary floor. Bennett, however, with drunken alacrity, rolled up and onto his feet and assaulted Bierce with a football tackle that cascaded the two inebriates into what became a pile of tables and chairs they knocked about recklessly in a raucous melee. The two staggered about with wanton abandon, kicking, punching and swearing, before the bouncer and the bartender descended upon them remorselessly, and manhandled them to the swinging doors before heaving them airborne, one after another, onto the thoroughfare. After rising from the dust to scream a caustic insult or two in each other's direction, the two went their separate ways, seeking out the after-hours emporiums that were closer to Hell's Kitchen.

\* \* \* \* \* \* \*

Charles Dana was, by this time, retired from the Sun and a widower, living with his oldest son and children. He still longed for the days when he was all powerful at his newspaper, however, especially now with the Spanish American War. On this day his teenage grandson, home while his parents were away, had showed his father a copy of the Journal, with its rabble rousing narration of the patriotic war. This dramatic page had a big effect on the old man's demeanor, and he attempted to escape his confinement to get back to the Sun. He rattled the locked screen door at the front of the residence.

"Someone open this door for me," he cried out desperately. "I have got to get down to the paper. They need me!"

His nurse/caretaker sailed in from the rear of the house to steer the old man in another direction.

"It's okay, Mr. Dana," she cajoled him, "your employees will take care of it."

"They need me, damn it, let me go. The country is at war."

Gently but firmly, she led him back into the residence.

"We'll send a telegram, Mr. Dana. That will help, you can give them full instructions."

"They need me."

Truth be told, they did not feel they needed him and, as the years had gone on, Dana was pushed into a forced retirement as his guidance of the paper had grown more and more irrational.

"Come on, Mr. Dana, we know that you are retired."

Dana relented, and trudged back toward his study.

"It's not fair," he lamented.

"Please have a seat, Mr. Dana, and I'll make you some tea. Let me get you some paper to write your telegram."

"I've got it here somewhere," he cried out, fumbling around his desk.

The nurse cruised past Dana's grandson, accosting him on the way by.

"How many times do I have to tell you not to show him the newspapers?!"

The young man smirked.

\* \* \* \* \* \* \* \*

At the World that day, things were not going well for Pulitzer. Once again, Hearst had snookered Pulitzer with one of the tricks that Pulitzer himself had used on his competition years ago, and the old man felt flummoxed. White read to him from a front page story in the Journal as he sat listening, ashen faced.

"Reflipe W. Thenuz was a trick story, dear readers, to test the news gathering methods of Mr. Pulitzer. The same letters, as you can probably see, spell we pilfer the news. Pulitzer, as he has done frequently, has stolen stories from the Journal, being unable to report real stories in his own paper, so we used this fictitious story to prove it."

Just as Pulitzer had tricked the Republican in St. Louis many years ago, Hearst had laid a trap for him.

"Didn't someone check the facts on this story?!"

"No," mumbled White.

"He's using all of my own little tricks against me," moaned Pulitzer. "John was right, I've lowered us down to Hearst's level, and the more we try to fight him the lower we go. It's like fighting Satan himself."

Suddenly a loud rattling noise came from down the hall, and the silent and somber World employees looked in that direction, and beheld Ambrose Bierce, whose face bore the scars of his recent bar room altercation, emerging from a lengthy struggle with the sliding metal mesh door of the elevator. He struggled to gain his balance, and then began to boldly tramp toward his confrontation with Joseph Pulitzer in the newsroom.

"I am here to bring you greetings from William Randolph Hearst, Pulitzer, and to congratulate you on your recent stealth of a fake news story."

"And who the hell are you?!" blared Pulitzer.

"It's Ambrose Bierce," White whispered in Pulitzer's ear.

"Ah, Mr. Bierce, the Hearst hit man."

White motioned to the back of the Dome for assistance.

"Your opinion of me is becoming irrelevant, Pulitzer, because you are finished in the news business."

"Who the hell are you to tell me something like that, Bierce, you're just a bit player in Hearst's newspaper circus."

"Circus, you jealous old fart?! You weren't in the ring, obviously, when we took on the Leland Stanford railroad octopus in California."

"I've done more than you..."

"Hardly," blared Bierce. "You're only in two cities and we're all across the country. We help more people every day than you ever helped in your entire career."

"Hearst is only out for himself, you bozo-"

"And what about you? You're a sideshow now, Pulitzer, admit it, the train has passed you by. Your day in the sun has come and gone."

This assault on his status as a newsman was too much for Pulitzer, who stood up, shaking in rage.

"I've taken all I am going to take from you and your boss, Bierce. Get your ass over here and I will tear you limb from limb!"

He leaped forward clumsily, attempting to find Bierce.

"My goodness, he wants to fight," chortled Bierce.

Pulitzer threw his sunglasses to the floor behind him, and stomped toward where he heard the voice of Bierce.

"Come on, you punk!"

"Mr. Pulitzer, please," White pleaded.

Bierce pranced to his right, to avoid the lunging Pulitzer, and put his fists up with the back of his hands facing forward, sarcastically imitating the classic boxing pose.

"All right, let's go, Marquis of Queensbury rules. Get 'em up, Pulitzer."

Pulitzer thrashed out at where he heard Bierce's voice, but, again, he danced out of the way.

"Stay in one place, you weasel!"

"Your boxing pose is not very intimidating, Mr. Pulitzer."

"I am going to get you, Goddamnit!"

Pulitzer swung wildly again and, once more, Bierce pranced aside to avoid the blow. The aging editor lost his balance and cried out in anguish as he fell to the floor, where he lay in a twitching heap at Bierce's feet.

"He's down, ladies and gentlemen, Pulitzer is down. Who's going to do the ten count?"

Victor Cole finally arrived from the press room in the basement, and seized Bierce by the belt and collar to drag him away.

"Have you taken to picking on senior citizens, Mr. Bierce?"

Bierce was not shut up by this admonition, and cried out in defiance as he was dragged down the hallway.

"My goodness, they've called the bouncer. Well, Pulitzer, you're through, face it, your day has come and gone! So long, has been!"

As Bierce was dragged away employees carefully carried the listless Pulitzer to a leather couch and gently placed him upon it. He lay there silently, gradually regaining his senses, resting quietly, until Doctor McClane, a nurse and an orderly appeared to place him upon a stretcher and bear him homeward. As he was being carried away, he addressed his employees in a farewell.

"He is right! What can I say? I have been beaten at my own game, buried by an avalanche I myself created. But what did I expect? To rule the world always and forever? Apparently, like many of the world's idealists, I had foolish expectations. It is time for me to realize that all paths to glory, as the Great Bard says, lead but to the grave. And so, ladies and gentlemen, it is time for me to let other men take their turn at the helm. Do not despair, the battle will go on. But my day is done, as they say, so I bid you all a fond farewell."

The old master was taken into the elevator where the sliding door closed him off, and Joseph Pulitzer departed the scene.

\* \* \* \* \* \* \* \*

Back in the living room of his New York home the next day, Pulitzer sat quietly in his pajamas, as his old friend Thomas Davidson counseled him. Davidson had the emotional access to Pulitzer that few could match, as the irascible news editor kept most people at a healthy distance. This was an especially low period for Pulitzer, as the cruel world had made it apparent that he, the man who had considered himself a gallant knight who could slay the evil dragons of the world with a mighty slashing sword, the man who did not fear confrontations from men all the way from Captains of Industry to Tammany Hall—this gallant man no longer had the power he once had, and must retreat back into the solitary world of secretaries, letters and cables of which it was his plight to be a prisoner.

"Yes, Joseph, you have opened the floodgates of everyman's news."

"For good or for ill," Pulitzer responded.

"Oh come on, Joseph, don't be silly. You've woken people up to enormous problems of inequality in American life, and you've changed the way newspapers operate. Look at the difference you're brought about. For starters, the rich are finally being taxed to help the less fortunate, which never would have happened if you hadn't made a stink about it."

"I suppose," moaned the invalid.

"Joseph please," chimed in Kate, "don't be so hard on yourself. You've done a lot of good."

Ponsonby discreetly rounded the corner from the hallway to the entrance.

"Mr. Schurz is here to see you, Mr. Pulitzer."

Pulitzer took a moment to respond.

"Send him in."

Schurz trod slowly around the corner and, though Pulitzer did what little he could to hide it, tears had come to his eyes.

"Joseph, Joseph, Joseph."

"Hello, Carl."

"I've come to apologize, Joseph. I have been a little hard on you lately."

"Thank you."

"You just have to tame down the reporters a little bit."

"Yes, Carl. And, I suppose, hire John Cockerill back, if he'll come."

There was a moment of silence

"Buck up, Joseph," Davidson interjected. "I'm sure there will be other challenges."

\* \* \* \* \* \* \*

# Chapter 9

## **The Final Battle**

And so Pulitzer retreated back into his solitary world. Kate and their two daughters, Edith and Constance, came to see him off at the pier when he boarded his yacht to sail off into seclusion. His daughters looked beautiful in their sporty white dresses, seated in a handsome cabriolet pulled by two impressive black mares.

"Good bye, my darling," said Kate, kissing him, "and write to me as often as you can."

"Bye, Daddy," said Constance as she kissed him.

And the women watched as Pulitzer's yacht pulled off and the aging news editor floated away with Ponsonby, Dr. Hosmer and his team of secretaries in his aquatic sound-proofed lair.

It had been decided, with Pulitzer's reluctant consent, for him to take a trip around the world as a way to enable him to find peace of mind while separated from his worldly obsessions. The secretarial team crossing the Atlantic kept him somewhat free from boredom by reading Shakespeare. They chose Much Ado About Nothing and other comedies, thinking this might be the best way to keep the aging man in good spirits. This worked for a time, but as they approached the coast of England Pulitzer returned his attention to more earthly matters— Presidential politics, to be exact. The 1900 Presidential election was coming up, and the old man could not shed his addiction to having a major say in who the next President would be. So when his boat docked temporarily in Liverpool a secretary was sent into town to pick up his correspondence, along with all the copies of the World and the competing papers that Pulitzer had arranged to be sent there. His team was overloaded with work keeping Pulitzer up to date on world events and the mountainous flow of letters and telegrams back and forth from the old master to his employees.

"They cannot nominate that bum again, Goddamnit!" Pulitzer wailed out, after hearing news about the initial efforts of William Jennings Bryan to get the Democratic Party nomination again. "He does not have the interests of the Democratic Party at heart! Besides that, he will never get elected, no matter how many times they nominate him. The farmers and miners do not have enough votes to elect a President."

"Be that as it may, Mr. Pulitzer," said Ponsonby, "he controls the party machinery."

Ponsonby was right, and Pulitzer could not deny it, for Bryan was very popular in the western United States. Having galvanized the Democratic Party Convention in 1896 with his Cross of Gold speech, where he demanded that the dollar be taken off of the Gold Standard, Bryan had swept his way to the nomination only to lose resoundingly to William McKinley in the general election.

"Why should they let a man control the party machinery who cannot ever win the Presidential election?!" Pulitzer bellowed.

He was bitter about this man leading the Democratic Party in the opposite direction he believed it should take. He had thought that Grover Cleveland had awakened the Democrats and made them turn the corner toward the immigrants and the cities, their true constituency, the constituency that could elect them. When Bryan appeared, Pulitzer thought, perhaps wishfully, that he was but an apparition, with no long term support. Pulitzer had met him once, in Maine, when the candidate from Nebraska had come up to gain his endorsement, and Pulitzer thought him a nice and honorable man, but misguided. Pulitzer predicted almost exactly the states that Bryan could carry in the general election, and knew that in the 1900 election, if re-nominated, he may not even be able to carry all of those.

"Dewey, Goddamn it, Dewey!" Pulitzer proclaimed.

He was referring to Admiral George Dewey, who had suddenly become a very popular man. In the Philippines, at the Battle of Manila, he had bombed and obliterated the wooden Spanish Navy ships in that remote part of the Spanish American War. This military triumph was so well received that Dewey had returned to a hero's reception in New York City. He had become the talk of the town, and the subject of a national frenzy that included neckties with his name on them, bubble gum called Dewey Chewies and many babies named after him. As an instant celebrity, Pulitzer saw him as a man who could follow the tradition of a military hero turned politician who could become the savior of the Democratic Party, and had appealed to him to run for President. Unfortunately, one thing in the correspondence they picked up in Liverpool was a letter from Dewey stating that he thought he was too old, lacked the experience and had no desire to run for President. This was not the first time that Pulitzer had tried to enlist him, as he had previously sent a reporter to the Philippines for that purpose, who obtained the same response: Dewey felt he was too old, politically inexperienced, and had no desire to run.

"It looks like a lost cause," Ponsonby declared.

"We have got to keep trying, Claude."

And try he did, having a string of editorials written in New York and St. Louis endorsing Dewey for President. As Pulitzer's trip continued, perhaps Dewey was changing his mind. Some suspected that Dewey's new wife had something to do with it, a woman who perhaps had political ambitions of her own. Many analysts could come up with no other reason Dewey had suddenly changed his mind and became a candidate. Yet they judged from his first appearances as a candidate that perhaps he lacked the experience to run, as he had to be prodded in two separate interviews what political party he was a member of before, to Pulitzer's relief, he announced that he was a Democrat in the second interview. By that time, unfortunately, it was too late, for Dewey's star in the limelight was fading, and people no longer took him seriously. Besides that, the Primary Election season was about to begin, and Dewey had none of the campaign infrastructure needed to launch a major candidacy, so many political pundits made fun of him, and his candidacy seemed more like a joke. Joseph Pulitzer, and perhaps Dewey's wife, were very disappointed. But another military hero returned from the war whose political star was on the rise on a far more stable track.

\* \* \* \* \* \* \* \*

Colonel Theodore Roosevelt, as he was known following the Spanish American War, was on his way to a dock not far from the one from which Pulitzer had recently departed, and New York City was gearing up for a major league celebration. As the boats containing Roosevelt and his Rough Riders were approaching, sporadic chants of "Ted-dy! Ted-dy! Ted-dy!" were already echoing sporadically around lower Manhattan, where shoulder to shoulder crowds grew in strength as the public anticipated his arrival. The Colonel was a familiar figure in New York City, as he had been a Congressman, Police Commissioner and Mayoral Candidate in his years of residence there. Yet Roosevelt's popularity, following the Spanish American War, reached far beyond New York, as his military heroism with the Rough Riders had made him possibly the most popular man in the country. Just about any city in the nation could have matched the ticker tape parade that Roosevelt sparked upon Manhattan, and all Americans anxiously awaited news of the doings of this military hero they had so much cause to worship. When Roosevelt's cruise ship dropped down its gangplank upon the home country the shouts for Teddy seemed to shake the very earth on the small island of Manhattan, and valiant cries echoed about in worship of this valiant military man. Roosevelt rose to the challenge of the vibrant crowds that awaited him, and he flashed his famous pearly whites shamelessly while reaching out to both sides of the close cropped crowd to shake hands rapid fire all the way down to the open horse carriage that awaited him. Waving to the parade spectators and smiling valiantly— his Rough Riders marching in military formation behind him— Roosevelt rode up Broadway to City Hall, basking in the ecstatic adulation of the thick crowds. Then, as he mounted the steps to the stage to give out the patriotic welcome home speech he knew would be printed in newspapers across the country, his ascent was accompanied by, what else, Hearst-financed red white and blue fireworks. After the fireworks and the adulation of the crowd were quieted, his speech was appropriately non-political, about war and sacrifice and patriotism and dispelling evil regimes, and the crowd lapped it up. There were, as he knew, patriotic expectations amongst his listeners, for he was shortly to become a candidate for governor of New York State.

He soared into the office in one of the most lopsided gubernatorial campaigns in American history, as he was, without doubt, at that moment, the most popular man in the country. Speaking on train whistle stops throughout the state he charmed the people with his flashing teeth and oratorical bravado, accompanied by a few Rough Rider veterans who took on a role that was a cross between the secret service and dragoons for show. He was elected by a crushing landslide. But not quite everyone supported him, and his old enemy, Republican Boss Platt, was adamantly against him, and was unsure of what to do when this impetuous bad boy, in his opinion, became the Governor of New York State.

* * * * * * * *

Platt, we recall, was the boss of the Republican Party in New York State, and had a long history of conflict with Theodore Roosevelt. As the man who controlled the fund raising machinery for candidates for political office, Platt also controlled what bills were passed in Albany, as the Republican Party controlled the New York State Legislature in the late 1800s until past the turn of the century. At that time, far fewer Americans had a college education, and the vast majority of legislators in Albany were hard working good old boys with a firm loyalty to Boss Platt. When Theodore Roosevelt, fresh out of Harvard, showed up in Albany, he didn't fit in and was made fun of by his colleagues for his fancy clothes and upper crust accent. That didn't stop Roosevelt from proposing many bills that Platt and his machine hated, and Roosevelt was a man who could not be bought off or intimidated. Later as a Police Commissioner and Mayoral Candidate for New York City Roosevelt continued to refuse to bow down to Boss Platt, and had several very public encounters against him, some of which Roosevelt won, like the time as Police Commissioner he rallied the churches against him in the dispute about enforcing the saloon closures on Sundays. This victory cost Platt a lot of bribery cash from the saloons.

When Roosevelt became Governor-Elect, Platt wanted to get rid of him soon, and pulled strings in the party machinery to make that happen. He sat in his Albany office listening to Timothy Ellsworth, the Leader of the State Senate, relating to him Roosevelt's campaign appearances. Ellsworth, on Platt's orders, had placed one of his staff members on the train as an observer.

"He speaks from the caboose," Ellsworth informed him, "and there are crowds as far as the eye can see wherever he stops."

"They worship him," groaned Platt.

"And he's got those Rough Rider fellows with him, in their uniforms, surrounding the caboose like a Praetorian Guard."

"The speeches?"

"He sticks mostly to domestic stuff, Mr. Platt, and promises to knock down, as he terms them, the rich and powerful robber barons."

"Enough," gasped Platt, tired of hearing of the successes of a man he so detested, "we're going to get rid of him."

"Oh?" queried Ellsworth.

"We're going to kick his silk-stockinged ass upstairs."

"You're going to make him take the veil?" Ellsworth asked, referring to the slang term of the time for becoming Vice-President.

The analogy was about it being like becoming a Catholic nun, as the main duties of that office then would be attending state funerals and hoping that the President might die.

"Indeed."

"McKinley's not going to want him any more than you do."

"He'll take one for the team, Timothy," Platt predicted, "as he knows that we've got to get him somewhere where he can't get anything done."

"For the good of the Party and the country."

"Damn straight."

\* \* \* \* \* \* \* \*

Back on the yacht, Pulitzer was slightly less displeased than Platt about the rise of Roosevelt, though he took some self-satisfied pleasure in it, since he had predicted that the cowboy would use his war experience for his own political gain. Pulitzer had tried unsuccessfully to circumvent him by promoting Admiral Dewey to political prominence without success so he, like the rest of the world, would have to watch Roosevelt's political progress whether he liked it or not. Roosevelt was, to him, a conundrum, as Pulitzer regarded him as an immature war hawk on the foreign policy side while somewhat admiring him as he emerged as the self-styled Trust Buster, who would attack the robber barons that Pulitzer had severely criticized in his newspapers for decades. In doing so he was stealing issues that properly belonged to the Democrats though, and Pulitzer felt a deep resentment toward Roosevelt for that, and doubted whether Roosevelt, as a Republican, really meant what he said in that regard.

Pulitzer ordered the yacht to sidetrack from his supposed world tour by making a left hand turn into the Mediterranean, causing his secretarial team to suspect he had no intention of leaving the waters of Europe, and they were right. Pulitzer knew that once they traveled south of Gibraltar, along the coast of either Africa or South America, he would have scant access to either the mail or telegraph for extended periods. So rather than argue the point when the trip was proposed, Pulitzer used the stealth method, and took them on a tour of the Mediterranean for that fall where they stayed in Nice, Monaco, and Naples among other places. Thereafter Pulitzer's life resumed that of a lonely fugitive forever seeking quieter and more beautiful places, fleeing the bad weather, and forever in search of fresh interesting companionship on his secretarial team.

He had bought a new home in Jekyll Island, Georgia, where many of the same plutocratic families he had lived uncomfortably near on the East Side of Manhattan also had places. With his illnesses, such as diabetes, bronchitis, and rheumatism, among others, it was a constant struggle to find the right climate to make him the most comfortable. During cruises around the European Continent, he went to numerous spas and resorts, visiting some of the best doctors in the world. He desperately longed to find a medical expert to give him different advice, but it was always the same: don't work so much. This was like telling a lion not to hunt. So he created his own assembled world, with his places to go and secretaries to help him do his oh, so heavy workload.

Regarding his secretaries, the vast majority of the team were always British, as the position, with Pulitzer's temper tantrums and dictatorial behavior, required men who were more versed in a society with a class structure and ethics of duty and honor. Americans, temperamentally speaking, had a far more difficult time in such a subservient role. Long time employees of the World would often accompany Pulitzer on trips on the yacht but the secretaries spent the bulk of time with him, taking dictation, arranging for the meals and so on. The World employees were brought in at the proper time to be grilled about a whole host of things going on at the paper, and receiving relentless instructions that went even beyond the mountain of letters and telegrams that Pulitzer sent back daily.

Of all the hundreds of issues that Pulitzer dealt with in the last years of his life, there was one that stood out in importance in the history of American journalism, and that was a conflict he had with Theodore Roosevelt because it involved freedom of speech and freedom of the press, in a historic ruling before the Supreme Court. This was the final major battle of Pulitzer's long career.

Theodore Roosevelt, probably more than any other American President, seemed fated to hold that prestigious office. Elected to be governor in 1898 he did not stay in that position long, and Platt got him to take the veil, as it were, for the election of 1900. As Pulitzer had predicted, Williams Jennings Bryan lost badly once again in the rematch against McKinley, and Platt and others were relieved that they had the political bad boy out of the way, at least temporarily. It was temporarily, indeed, as the winds of fate would have it, and McKinley was shot by the mad anarchist Leon Czolgosz, and Theodore Roosevelt became President in 1901.

Pulitzer, still a sometimes lukewarm supporter of the man he termed the Cowboy President, went on with having his newspapers treat him with mixed reviews, with faint praise for his attacking the rich, and condemnations for his aggressive foreign policy.

"It seems like the he's always expected to become President," Pulitzer declared moodily to his secretarial team, crossing the Atlantic.

"Yet he will be the most essentially American President so far, don't you think, Mr. Pulitzer?" Ponsonby inquired.

"Perhaps," Pulitzer responded, "unless he is being an imposter."

"Imposter?" Dr. Hosmer inquired.

"Roosevelt comes from big money," Pulitzer replied, "much like an aristocrat."

"But his father made his own fortune," Ponsonby observed.

"True, but does Roosevelt want to help the poor? No. Does he want to tax the rich? No. He might say that he's going to do something to stop all those rich robber barons, but he takes money from them for his campaign chest. He might be doing all that just to get the votes, those bellicose campaign speeches where he promises to take them down, it's all balderdash."

"But look at his campaign style, the flashing teeth, the boyish grin, the incessant hand shaking, you can't imagine any English gentleman doing any of that," Ponsonby declared.

"True," Pulitzer conceded.

"And his almost childish warlike style to make himself a hero," Dr. Hosmer said, "very American."

"There I have to disagree with you, Doctor," Pulitzer cautioned. "The boy-like manner of his diplomatic pronouncements might seem new and American, but you can hardly call his imperialist desires original. He has America lining up behind the imperialists of Europe for the same Goddamned greed of empire that they have perfected through the years."

"But there is a difference, Mr. Pulitzer, between putting in a ruling class, as the British have all over the world, and just companies going in to make money."

"Only of degree," Pulitzer replied.

This line of Pulitzer's thought was firm regarding Roosevelt's foreign policy, and he instructed his papers to take a combative line against the aggressive foreign adventurism of the former Rough Rider, and the conflict between him and Theodore came to a head regarding the diplomacy of digging the Panama Canal.

The tale of the Panama Canal is one of adventure, intrigue, comedy, bullying, betrayal, bribery and con artists. Theodore Roosevelt took it upon himself to cut through this maze with bold action, including the diplomatic bravado in relation to other countries that Pulitzer most deplored. Many supporters of Roosevelt had a hand in the financial chicanery involving the investment leading up to its construction, but Roosevelt's brutish ambition to build the canal blinded him to such transgressions.

He filled up the Cooper Union Hall in Manhattan with Republican conservatives for one speech on the subject, a speech that made Carl Schurz shudder with disgust at what he regarded as an invasion of barbarians to this hallowed hall when he found out they leapt and cheered at such remarks as:

"You must know, ladies and gentlemen, that if we had a canal built before the Spanish American War we could have gotten our Navy ships to Cuba months faster than we did! [Wild cheers erupted from the audience] Do we need it for our national security? [Listeners stomped their feet in a wild crescendo of applause shouting the affirmative.] Absolutely, ladies and gentlemen, our path is clear, we must build this canal. It is not only for the huge gains in trade that will be great for our economy, but our national interest is at stake!" [A standing ovation followed.]

Pulitzer did not react well to the speech.

"Let's send out a wire to John Cockerill right away," Pulitzer instructed Ponsonby in his office at Jekyll Island. "It is not proper for the President of the United States to be a Rough Rider on the Bully Pulpit, predicting how he's going to intimidate the rest of the world!"

A canal through Central America was originally started by the French under Bernard de'Champs, but the difficulty of digging through the tropical jungles of Panama proved too costly and difficult, so the French government wanted to get rid of this boondoggle by foisting it off on the United States. Roosevelt did not feel it was a boondoggle and took up its implementation with a ruthless determination.

Not all Americans felt, however, that the canal should be dug in Panama. A study by a team of engineers had determined that it would be better to dig the canal in Nicaragua. Its path would be longer, it was true, but two large lakes could be used in its construction, making it a far easier choice than the dense jungles and mountainous terrain in the rainforests of Panama. Besides that, an investment in the Panama project required the United States to pay off some debts of the failed French project, and why take on that unnecessary expense? Because of these factors, the House of Representatives passed a Bill supporting the construction of the canal in Nicaragua. Many of the original investors in the Panama project, though, were supporters of Roosevelt, and they already had sunk millions into the French debacle, so the President could not deny them their just due. So Roosevelt's allies in Congress quickly came up with urgent reasons the canal should be dug in Panama.

Senator Mark Hanna, a wealthy robber baron entrepreneur who had won a Senate seat to protect his fellow robber barons, gave a memorable speech to his colleagues on the subject. First he put up a topographical map of Nicaragua which had several red dots on the tops of mountains, and the enlarged map guide informed the Senate audience these red dots were volcanoes.

"Imagine the fate of American workers," he warned them, "if any one of these volcanoes erupt and rained down molten lava upon them? Remember, a volcano in Nicaragua erupts every twenty two and a half days, and the peril to the proposed canal site is precipitous!"

The Senators nodded solemnly at the truth of this outright lie, and Hanna brought in further catastrophic news to solidify his case.

"You can see from this chart, my fellow Senators, that Nicaragua is especially prone to violent earthquakes. They do not occur quite as often as the volcanoes," he cried out with a straight face, "but every thirty one days is fairly often."

He motioned to an aide who put up a different map of Nicaragua with expanding circles to indicate earthquakes, and the number of circles was large around the lakes where the canal was proposed to be built.

"That the earthquakes are particularly large in number where the canal route is proposed. Do you imagine that the structure of the canal will remain intact during a violent earthquake? Certainly not, gentlemen, and the poor workers would be killed by the collapsing of the canal walls about them in events that are mathematically certain to take place."

Thereafter the Senate promptly voted to restore construction of the canal to Panama, and the House of Representatives promptly followed suit. The Roosevelt Administration authorized a forty million dollar payment to the French Government to take over their bankrupt project, a project with many investors who were on Roosevelt's political team. This is where Round One, of the controversy, if you will, occurred.

"Who are these payments to?!" Pulitzer inquired, "and what is the money for? Not even a two-year-old would believe that the money is actually going to the French Government, but rather to a bunch of broken investors who are friends of Theodore Roosevelt, Goddamnit!"

Pulitzer was upon his yacht steaming back from Jekyll Island, preparing for one of his infrequent stays in New York. Frank Cobb, a daring reporter that the World had stolen from the Detroit Free Press, promptly wrote a forceful editorial that accused the Roosevelt Administration of collusion with corrupt investors in the Panama Canal project, putting their investment needs ahead of the correct foreign policy process of the United States Government. Citing the ridiculous presentations of Senator Mark Hanna to approve the Panama project, Cobb asserted that Roosevelt would stop at nothing to make sure his friends got rich.

President Theodore Roosevelt was incensed by the editorial.

"Who does Joseph Pulitzer think he is?!" Roosevelt bellowed out to General Wood in the Oval Office. "I'm going to sue this unpatriotic fellow for libel!"

Roosevelt promptly wrote a long and angry pronouncement to Congress to that effect, asserting that no United States citizen, especially the owner of a newspaper, could insult the President with such vicious, unproven lies and get away with it. He would prosecute for libel. Unfortunately for Roosevelt, the Constitution did not allow him to do so, and he had to rely on the District Attorney of New York City to do so, a man named Travis Jerome. Jerome was a colorful fellow, an attorney who often chose cases to prosecute based on what would favor him politically rather than a strict and steady application of the law. Unfortunately, this is often the case with elected District Attorneys. Here, Jerome hated both Pulitzer and Roosevelt, so it was unpredictable which way he would go. The World had previously taken a picture of Jerome when he had his feet up on his desk and was asleep, and printed this telling photo on the front page of its Sunday edition, with a headline and story questioning the seriousness with which Jerome took his job. Many World employees had deep fears that the President might be able to follow through on the prosecution. What would Joseph Pulitzer do? Would he back down?

By this time Pulitzer was back in New York, at his 55th street residence. In the building that he had repeatedly bewailed was not noise free, he had made a significant change. An acoustics expert from Harvard University was brought in to supervise the construction of an annex in the rear of the building, in which Pulitzer would stay during his sojourns to New York. It had cork floors, triple paned glass and other modern embellishments to provide complete silence, and the secretarial team promptly named it the Vault. Several employees of the World, John Cockerill, Frank White, Frank Cobb and others, waited outside the Vault to be called in by the master; they felt like they were patients at a dentist's office, waiting to go back and sit in the chair for their drillings. Then, when he was done with each of them, he called them all together for a final conference, in which he said:

"The World, gentlemen, will not be muzzled— not by the President of the United States nor anybody else. Regardless of what Roosevelt thinks of what we have said we are not going to shrink from it, for the charges we have brought are true, and if the owner of our newspaper goes to jail for it, so be it! The World will not be muzzled. Go on now, do what you have to do, you have your instructions."

The staff members promptly stood up and returned to the World to do their assigned tasks.

The question was, would Jerome prosecute, and everyone waited on pins and needles to find out the answer to that question. This waiting went on for over a week, and the one who was most threatened, Joseph Pulitzer, kept a steely calm through it all. This was one of the odd inconsistencies about the great newsman. Though a secretary's too-loud crunching when chewing a piece of toast might send him off into the deep end, he could remain calm under pressures which might have other men tearing their hair out. Pulitzer sent someone to find out from the source, and Cockerill made an appointment to have lunch with Jerome to that effect.

Across the table at Delmonico's Jerome seemed to enjoy his position of power.

"You've sent your flunkies to follow me around and take inappropriate pictures," he declared, "but now that Mr. Pulitzer feels threatened I get to speak to one of the higher ups?"

"A suit from the President of the United States," Cockerill responded, "is a very serious thing, no matter who occupies that office."

"Too true."

"Well, what's it going to be?"

"I hope you've enjoyed stewing in your own juices," Jerome announced, "but I'm not going to prosecute."

Cockerill felt immensely relieved, and felt to himself that Jerome had decided that prosecuting a very popular newspaper owner was not in his best political interest.

"Have you decided, gentlemen?" the waiter inquired.

Pulitzer had won the First Round.

\* \* \* \* \* \* \* \*

Round Two, however, was far more intense, and involved some foreign policy decisions made by Roosevelt that made Pulitzer's blood boil.

In the early negotiations about the Panama Canal, Panama was not yet a country, but a province of Colombia. At that time only a narrow mountain path led down to the tropical isthmus, the main function of which was as a mail route to the mainland, since the Province of Panama was but a lowly backwater with no particular economic value. The proposed canal changed that, but the difference was not immediately clear, as the original French attempt resulted in over twenty-thousand laborers dying during its construction. Most of the dead were imported labor, from the West Indian Islands in the Caribbean, many of whom succumbed to tropical diseases such as malaria, yellow fever or dysentery. Industrial accidents, however, also claimed numerous lives, when train wrecks, explosions and mud slides took the lives of others. Funeral trains whose sole cargo were the dead routinely came down the tracks, and it must have seemed to the native population that building the canal was a cruel and absurd idea. Through all of this, however, independence from Colombia was a mere pipe dream for Panamanians, as they were but a small province of the comparatively powerful mainland.

President Theodore Roosevelt changed all of that however, because of what happened in the negotiations with Colombia over building the canal.

Philippe-Jean Bunau-Varilla, originally the chief engineer for the French project, became an emissary to Washington from Panama and negotiated a treaty for building the canal. The treaty outlined the payments to Colombia for the use of its land for the canal, and Roosevelt was eager to begin its digging soon. The Colombian government, however, threw a wrench into the works when their Senate refused to ratify the treaty and asked for an additional ten million dollars to allow construction of the canal. This decision brought about both financial and publicity problems for Roosevelt, major obstacles, it would seem, to prevent him from building the canal.

"Oh this is rich!" William Randolph Hearst declared, never one to miss inflammatory news.

"Indeed it is," Ambrose Bierce declared.

"What is that fellow's name?" Hearst inquired. "Bunau-Varilla?"

"Banana-Vanilla," Bierce quipped.

"Hee-hee," Hearst laughed, "how about this for a headline, Bogota Stomps on the Banana-Vanilla Treaty?"

So Hearst, fickle semi-supporter of the President that he was, belittled Roosevelt's efforts to build the canal. Theodore Roosevelt, however, took bold action to bulldoze these problems out of the way.

"I am not going to let some Third World country push me around!" he swore to General Wood in the Oval Office.

"It seems like a difficult problem," his Chief of Staff declared.

"There are rumors that Panama wants to break off from Colombia anyway, are there not?"

"Yes sir, Mr. President."

"Well now they have perfectly legitimate reasons to do so, and it won't cost us ten million dollars!"

And so the creation of the nation of Panama began to be put in place, as Roosevelt sent down military advisors to the lowly province, telling them that their dreams of their own nation would come true. Money for bribes was freely dispensed, including twenty-five thousand dollars for the Panamanian Military Commander to order his troops to help foment a revolution. He was assured that the United States would support them with military aid, and that powerful ships from the United States with troops were just about to be on the way. On top of all that, the wife of Bunau-Varilla was sewing an inspirational flag for the new nation.

* * * * * * * *

Pulitzer, with ears to the ground about the actions of the Administration, was looking far more deeply than Hearst into the goings on in Panama, and Roosevelt's plans regarding the Panama Canal got him excited in ways that his doctors did their utmost to prevent.

"Gunboat diplomacy!" Pulitzer exclaimed to Ponsonby at his desk up in Maine. "It's Goddamn gunboat diplomacy!"

"You might call it that," Ponsonby affirmed.

"Here's what we're going to do, Claude. We're going to get Arthur Brisbane on a train down to Miami right away. We've still got that boat down there we used to ferry news reports in and out of Cuba, do we not?"

"Yes sir," Mr. Pulitzer.

"Brisbane is going to go down to Panama and find out the nuts and bolts of what that Goddamned Rough Rider is going to do."

"Very good, Mr. Pulitzer."

In Panama, Brisbane got into contact with the Panamanian rebels, and found out the details of the upcoming revolution. Colombia had gotten wind of the incipient rebellion, and sent ten thousand troops down to quell it. If left unchecked, there would be a civil war of sorts between the Colombian Army and the company of the newly constituted army of Panama that was evolving with bribery and supervision by Roosevelt's representatives. Brisbane found out through word of mouth in the cantinas with the Panamanian troops, the basics of what they expected, for these soldiers would not risk their lives in a war against their mother country without substantial support from the United States. Roosevelt sent American Marines down there to back them up, and the first arrived weeks before Panama was scheduled to declare independence on November 3, 1903. At that point, it was a difficult decision for the government of Colombia whether or not to fight the battle. They did not want to be humiliated by the United States, but found losing a war to them even more frightening. To seal the deal Roosevelt had three American destroyers and a troop transport ship carrying ten thousand Marines scheduled to arrive shortly before Panama declared independence. These ships would sail close to the Panamanian coast, and make the Colombian Army have second thoughts about suppressing the revolution.

So the World published a headline and a story about the Panamanian Revolution. The headline declared: GUNBOAT DIPLOMACY!!! The sub-headline beneath it read: US TROOPS TO ARRIVE IN PANAMA TOMORROW.

\* \* \* \* \* \* \* \*

President Theodore Roosevelt was madder than a recently caged tiger when he read the subversive headlines of the World.

"Who does this blabbermouth Hungarian think he is?!" he exclaimed, shaking the windows of the Oval Office. "He's letting America's enemies know about our military plans before they happen!"

"That he is," Captain Wood affirmed.

"If this isn't treason I don't know what is," Roosevelt declared, his huge white molars grinding in anger. "We have more than enough reason to charge him with libel now!"

Now that Roosevelt was able to charge Pulitzer with the Federal charge of treason, a grand jury was convened in Washington to look into the situation, and many World reporters and editors, including Brisbane and Cockerill, were summoned to be witnesses before it. Charges of libel and treason were brought against Joseph Pulitzer, and Roosevelt had the Justice Department put the case on ultra-high priority. Pulitzer directed the World's editorial position be that the issue was freedom of speech and freedom of the press, not libel or sedition. If the press was not free to criticize the President, then what was the purpose of the press, he questioned. Sailing on his yacht to get away from the emotional pressure that his doctors constantly warned him about, Pulitzer put up a front of determination, stoically maintaining that the case did not bother him in the least. But his secretaries and Kate knew better, for the threat of the possibility he might have to go to jail was real this time, should he lose the decision in this important case with the charge of treason.

The first Federal Court ruled in Pulitzer's favor, and declared that since war had not been declared, treason was not an issue, and that freedom of the press was more important than Roosevelt's complaints about Pulitzer maligning him. Roosevelt blamed that decision on what he termed liberal judges appointed by Grover Cleveland, and appealed the case, putting it on the fast track to the Supreme Court. The other newspapers could no longer ignore this historic case as it came up for trial. Involving basic issues of freedom of speech and freedom of the press, it was in their interest to root for Pulitzer whether or not they liked the free advertising he was getting from the trial.

\* \* \* \* \* \* \* \*

On the day of the trial before the Supreme Court, Theodore Roosevelt made a very grand entrance. The athletic Rough Rider bounded up the cement stairs to the Court, leaving his lawyers and even Secret Service Members in the dust, but stopped near the top to talk to reporters who beseeched him for a statement.

"When he opposed my candidacy for Mayor of New York, I let it pass. When he made fun of my crime fighting efforts as Police Commissioner, I shrugged and let it go. When he called me a warmonger as Assistant Secretary of the Navy, I let him have his opinion. But, fellow Americans, when he publicizes national secrets and tries to direct American foreign policy from his newspaper it is going too far, and I, for one, am going to do something about it."

Roosevelt turned on his heel to enter the court as the reporters unsuccessfully blurted out questions toward him. Pulitzer entered the courtroom more discreetly, arriving in an automobile to the entrance the court afforded to those celebrities who wanted to escape harassment by the press. Inside the courtroom, Oliver Wendell Holmes, then the Chief Justice, sat in the center with his impressive handlebar mustache distinguishing him from his fellow Justices, who looked down upon the parties. Seated on the right side of the Court, with his attorneys, Pulitzer cut an impressive figure. Despite his almost total blindness he was dressed to the nines in a formal suit, was meticulously groomed, and had the erect carriage of a very dignified man. Roosevelt's attorney, on the far side of the chamber, rose to make his final statement. These oral arguments were to supplement the written briefs required from both parties.

"The President of the United States, Your Honor, has the constitutional right to direct American foreign policy. When newspapers publish secret information that makes the President's intentions clear to our adversaries, it is treason. Mr. Pulitzer has clearly broken the law. State secrets are state secrets, Your Honor, and if they are going to be leaked and broached by someone untrained in the intricacies of foreign policy, the United States will be at the mercy of dictators of the world. Our nation must put an end to such dangerous behavior."

Roosevelt's lawyer sat down, and the Court was silent with expectation.

"Mr. Pulitzer?" Chief Justice Holmes inquired.

Pulitzer rose to his feet to make his own statement.

"What the President's attorney does not mention, your honor, is a very important part of the Constitution called the Bill of Rights. There is guaranteed the right to free speech and freedom of the press. The World has merely exposed the dishonesty and shenanigans that our President has engaged in so that he could build the canal he was so determined to build. President Roosevelt, your honor, tramped on the rights of a sovereign nation, Colombia, and engineered a revolution with gunboat diplomacy. No American is above the law, your honor, and it is very important that we have free speech and freedom of the press in order to restrain the power of the President. President Roosevelt wants to silence me, Your Honor, because he is ashamed of his actions, and if I were him, I, too, would be ashamed."

\* \* \* \* \* \* \* \*

Pulitzer fled to his yacht and took off to avoid winter weather at his house in Jekyll Island, then sailed back up to New York in the spring in anticipation of Supreme Court. Pulitzer wanted to appear at the World, and sought to do so when the Supreme Court decision was due to come down. Not having been warned of his appearance, an icy silence slid over the newsroom from the employees' shock at his appearance, and the great man emerged from the clattering sliding cage of the elevator, and strutted down the hallway toward the editing room as though he had 20/20 vision. He did not, however, and was about to crash into a newly installed telephone booth before Ponsonby yanked him to his left to avoid it.

"What did you do that for, you clumsy oaf?!" Pulitzer exclaimed.

"Mr. Pulitzer! What a pleasure!"

"John Cockerill, my old friend," Pulitzer exclaimed, his seeing ears having detected the voice of his old comrade, "now tell me, right away, what is your idea for the special story for tomorrow's front page."

This was a long practice at both the World and the Post-Dispatch, to everyday have a new and interesting story to capture readers' attention at the bottom of the front page, and the subject had to be something different than what had been prevalent in the news.

"Oh I can't wait to publish it, Mr. Pulitzer. Did you know that George McClellan, Jr., is gearing up for a run for mayor?"

"You don't say, that's wonderful, tell me all about it!"

So the two old friends strolled into Cockerill's office, and the newsroom somewhat returned to normal, but the employees could not shed their nervousness with the mysterious great magnate there in person. After a time Victor Cole appeared from downstairs, clad in his usual workman's clothes from the printing office.

He had been outside the telegraph office when the crucial message came in from the Supreme Court, and, old hand in the corporation that he was, they gave it to him to bring up to Mr. Pulitzer.

"Victor, my old friend! Great to see you!" Pulitzer exclaimed, walking out of Cockerill's office to stand before the newsroom. "Could you read us all the telegram, please John?"

Cockerill promptly opened up the telegram and, clearing his throat in preparation, broadcast its content to the anxious workers of the World.

"The Supreme Court has decided unanimously in favor of Joseph Pulitzer as the defendant in the case brought by President Theodore Roosevelt!"

The newsroom erupted in pandemonium as the workers, despite whatever misgivings some may have had about their very unusual owner, suddenly felt an emotional bond with him. Hoots, cheers, and whoops erupted among the dozens of people in and around the editing room in the nexus of the World in the Dome, and everyone felt a feeling of accomplishment, validation, that all their efforts were part of a great noble effort to make the world a better place. When the explosion died down, and paper cups of champagne were passed around, Pulitzer addressed them.

"As I am sure you all know, this suit is more than just about me, and more than just about us. The suit is about freedom of speech and freedom of the press, and the necessity of a fundamental part of the freedom of American democracy. It is very, very necessary, for the press to have the freedom to criticize the elected leaders of our republic, for without such criticism we will not have a democratic country. We, meaning the press, ladies and gentlemen, have become the Fourth Estate, and a very necessary part of American democracy."

A brief burst of applause welled up.

"Now about the World. As you should know, the World is a very catholic paper. What do I mean by that? I don't mean religion. The word catholic is a word that a certain church appropriated, and the meaning of the word itself is all-encompassing—including everybody—and that is the sense that I am using the term in. The World is a paper for everybody, from the lowest of the working class to the highest of the upper crust. Some in the upper crust, as you are well aware, are too snobby to read the World, and many think they get more out of inferior papers like the boring old Tribune."

A chorus of boos erupted.

"Our job in the future is to disabuse anyone of these notions and get everyone to read our paper, and get rid of the undemocratic notion that some people deserve better newspapers than others. Such thinking is aristocratic and un-American in nature, and we are the ones publishing a paper that tells the truth, criticizes leaders when necessary, provides entertainment and, most importantly puts the thrill of life into peoples' veins the moment they pick it up. The sacred duty of a newspaper is to provide for the people a feeling of connection with the great and vibrant world in which they live."

Restrained applause broke out.

"I must leave you now, ladies and gentlemen, and it is an honor to work with all of you. As most all of you know, you will be hearing from me."

Most everyone, familiar with their boss's voluminous correspondence to them, nodded meaningfully as Pulitzer began his trek toward the elevator, and the employees saw him off with applause again, some voicing cheers toward the man they well knew to be their fearless leader.

This was the final time that Pulitzer would visit his twenty storied World Building, which had once been the wonder of 1890.

\* \* \* \* \* \* \* \*

Two years later, Pulitzer, in his yacht, was relaxing in the early spring off of the coast of Normandy, France, when another yacht laid anchor fifty yards away. Pulitzer's crew paid the craft little notice until a man appeared to be approaching from there in a rowboat, so Ponsonby was called on deck to appraise the situation. No word was made to Pulitzer about it, who was listening to Dr. Hosmer read to him in German from a history of the Franco-Prussian War.

"Who in God's name could this be?" Ponsonby questioned incredulously.

Dr. Hosmer also came on deck, and they continued to peer downward, with little evidence of the man's identity as he was rowing with his back toward them. It was in the late afternoon, and the sea was fairly calm, the mid-day winds dying down as evening approached. The skiff turned sideways as it got close to Pulitzer's boat, and the man wore a rather impressive Fu-Manchu mustache.

"If I live and breathe, it is James Gordon Bennett," Ponsonby announced. "Stall him, I'll break the news."

Pulitzer cold shouldered the interruption in his historical studies.

"Completely unannounced!" he exclaimed.

"This is one of the disadvantages of not having a wireless aboard, sir," Ponsonby said sheepishly.

Pulitzer had agreed not to have wireless devices installed to give him less access to communication to ease his nerves.

"I'll see him on deck Goddamnit," Pulitzer snarled. "Put out a few of the canvass chairs."

So Pulitzer received his guest somewhat politely, and the two sat together looking landward on the starboard side of the boat. They discussed various goings on in the newspaper business.

"Ambrose Bierce, I am afraid, came to a somewhat untimely end," Bennett informed him.

"Suicide?" Pulitzer queried.

"Not quite."

"Do tell."

"He strapped on a money belt with twelve hundred dollars in it, and wandered across the border into Mexico."

"That does sound suicidal."

"Hearst was castle shopping in England when he took off, so he didn't get a word about it until a month later."

"Oh?" Pulitzer queried.

"They sent out a search team who spent a month looking and could not find hide nor hair of him."

"Probably in shallow grave at the nearest cantina to the border."

"I think his ashes are at the bottom of a large bonfire along with a few bottles of tequila," Bennett theorized.

The two sat silent for a minute.

"I read your obituary of Charles Dana the other day," Bennett remarked.

"Oh?" Pulitzer inquired.

"It seemed odd that you were so very kind to him."

"Why shouldn't I be?"

"Mr. Pulitzer, all of us newspaper owners, as you know, have had fights, from time to time, but he was especially mean to you."

"Well, Mr. Bennett, he was old and did not have his full faculties at that point, so I see no point in having him judged in that regard."

"That's very kind of you."

Again, they sat silent for a minute.

"Are we going to have a drink?" Bennett inquired.

"I'm sorry, Mr. Bennett, my drinking days are over, just a sip of wine now and then. I also do not have my full faculties you know."

"Ha!" Bennett exclaimed. "Usually you don't let that stop you."

The two laughed.

"Ah well then, I have to be off. Thank you kindly for receiving me on such short notice."

"Don't mention it, Mr. Bennett, it was a pleasure to see you."

As soon as Bennett was out of ear-shot, Pulitzer muttered.

"He pretended to be friendly."

"Yes Sir," Ponsonby remarked.

"You seemed to get on handsomely, Mr. Pulitzer."

"The operative word in that sentence, Claude, is seemed."

"Indeed."

They sat silent for a minute.

"There's one more telegram for today", Mr. Pulitzer."

"Oh?"

He pulled it out of his pocket.

"It is from Mr. Hearst. It is an invitation to come and visit him at his castle in San Simeon, California."

"Oh that's a hoot. He wants me to come up and visit him with his private zoo and transported castle paraphernalia from Europe."

"It's a very popular spot for the entertainment crowd out west, Sir."

"Perhaps we could bring Bennett along and we could all get drunk."

"Indubitably," Ponsonby refrained.

"A crazy place for some crazy people," Pulitzer lamented. "The world is changing, Claude."

"Indeed it is, Mr. Pulitzer."

So Pulitzer lived on until his death with his secretarial team roaming about the earth in the seclusion of his own artificially created world. Despite the great challenges of working with him none of his long time secretaries, and there were dozens, regretted the experience.

They felt it was an honor to assist such a dynamic and brilliant man, and were grateful to have been afforded the honor of knowing him so intimately.

\* \* \* \* \* \* \* \*

So, now that we are at the end of our little story, who was Joseph Pulitzer?

He was a man with a fascinating life, who came to America as an angry seventeen-year-old who barely spoke English, yet developed and owned two major papers in the country some twenty years later. Despite numerous challenges, including poverty and anti-Semitism, he succeeded, and not only did he succeed but he brought out a new and different kind of journalism. He reached out to people who had not previously read newspapers, connecting with them on a gut level that raised their expectations of their own fate. It was odd that, as an immigrant, he brought about a very American cultural revolution, and helped to shake the ground under the powers-that-be that changed the whole tone of political life. Pulitzer was ahead of his time, politically, and pushed the Democratic Party toward the inner-city constituents they would not marshal until some twenty years after his death in 1911. Many issues that he pushed for were accomplished in the Progressive Era, not long after he passed away, such as an end to child labor, an income tax, legalization of labor unions and workplace safety laws. All of these were on the list of reforms he put on the front page in an early edition of the World, when people could not believe that they would ever happen, but they did.

On a personal level, Pulitzer had some problems that are a telling lesson to those of us with great ambitions to change the world. His physical constitution could not handle the ruthless demands put upon it by his soaring ambitions, which caused him to have a breakdown that left him with severe limitations for the rest of his earthly life. He overcame these physical obstacles to still exert meticulous control of his newspapers and have a big impact on the newspaper industry until his death. Only during the Spanish American War did he, because of the circulation war with Hearst, descend into rabble rousing journalism on which his and Hearst's careers are sometimes unfairly judged. Hearst and Pulitzer both did a lot of important things to rein in the unfettered capitalism of their day which was very unfair to many Americans. The problem Pulitzer had, however, was that his newspapers depended on his almost complete control of all their functions at almost all times. There were rarely any complaints about Pulitzer's management style, though, especially among his most senior employees, who were awed by his intelligence in every missive he sent to them about their newspaper work. After the great man's death, however, the World faded away into bankruptcy without Pulitzer there to guide it anymore, and only the Post-Dispatch remains in the newspaper business, as a legacy of his greatness. Perhaps his goal was too ambitious, in wanting to have a newspaper that everyone would read, from the lowest street sweeper to the richest businessman. Today, publishers would consider that goal impossible, as the New York Times is a whole different kettle of fish than the Daily News, and never the twain will meet.

The main thing he is remembered for today, the Pulitzer Prizes, were an entity he created in his final years. His purpose in creating them was to ensure that excellence was maintained in the public sphere of news, information and entertainment and having awards to reward them. Some might consider it ironic, today, that a man who would not even allow his own reporters to have bylines, created such awards for people to help proclaim their own greatness. For Pulitzer, despite all of his problems, firmly believed that it was the duty of the individual to do his utmost to help out the many who were far less fortunate than himself. He accomplished that goal in his own life, and felt that others should do the same. Though he was not a religious man he went out of his way to promote one of the most fundamental aspects of the Judeo-Christian philosophy, that the primary way to love God was to love and help your neighbor more than you love and help yourself.

The End

Made in the USA
Middletown, DE
18 August 2017